Novellas:

Lady Sophia's Rescue
Christmas Brides (3 Regency Novellas)

American Historical Romance

A Summer to Remember (3 American Historical Romances)

World War II Romance

It Had to be You

Inspirational Regency Romance

Marriage of Inconvenience

Political intrigue and suspense...

As speech writer to the Texas lieutenant governor, lovely Lacy Blair accidentally stumbles onto a high-level fraud involving state funds and masterminded by her boss. Since she can't risk snooping into the situation herself, she secretly consults with an FBI agent who agrees to help her investigate. Soon afterwards, she realizes she is being watched, and the FBI agent has been killed.

Terrified for her own safety and hungry for justice, she flees. But where can she turn? Who can she trust? Her former lover, Mike Talamino, is the only person she could ever count on. But will he agree to help her? Can she endanger him, too?

Texas Heroines in Peril Series

Capitol Offense is part of the contemporary romantic suspense series, *Texas Heroines in Peril*. As the series title suggests, each installment will focus on a Texas heroine in danger in a different locale. *Capitol Offense* is based in San Antonio and Austin with Texas politics as the background. *Protecting Britannia* finds the Texas heroine framed for murder in London while on an antique buying trip. *Murder at Veranda House*'s young widow heroine is forced to turn her Galveston Island home into a B&B after the mysterious death of her husband. In *A Cry in the Night* the Texas heroine desperately searchers for the son she put up for adoption years earlier and who is now in danger.

To Take This Lord (**Brides of Bath, Book 4**)
(originally titled An Improper Proposal)
"Bolen does a wonderful job building simmering sexual tension between her opinionated, outspoken heroine and deliciously tortured, conflicted hero." – *Booklist of the American Library Association*

My Lord Wicked
Winner, International Digital Award for Best Historical Novel of 2011.

A Duke Deceived
"A Duke Deceived is a gem. If you're a Georgette Heyer fan, if you enjoy the Regency period, if you like a genuinely sensuous love story, pick up this first novel by Cheryl Bolen." – *Happily Ever After*

One Golden Ring
"*One Golden Ring*...has got to be the most PERFECT Regency Romance I've read this year." – *Huntress Reviews*

Holt Medallion winner for Best Historical, 2006

The Counterfeit Countess
Daphne du Maurier award finalist for Best Historical Mystery

"This story is full of romance and suspense. . . No one can resist a novel written by Cheryl Bolen. Her writing talents charm all readers. Highly recommended reading! 5 stars!" – *Huntress Reviews*

"Bolen pens a sparkling tale, and readers will adore her feisty heroine, the arrogant, honorable Warwick and a wonderful cast of supporting characters." – *RT Book Reviews*

Capitol Offense

(Texas Heroines In Peril)

Cheryl Bolen

Harper & Appleton

Chapter 1

The cab stopped in front of the Alamo. It was the only place Lacy Blair could think of to tell the driver. She'd been to San Antonio a few times, not long enough to master any street names but long enough to soak in the city's colorful Mexican influences. Not that those colorful influences crossed her mind today. Only one thing was on her mind.

Staying alive.

She felt certain no one would be able to trace her here, and that knowledge might just ease her mind long enough for her to devise a plan of survival.

She paid the fare and fell into step with the throngs. If her memory served her correctly, the river's big mall was a few hundred yards from the Alamo. That must be where all the tourists were headed.

Within two minutes she was inside the three-story shopping center. River Center was its name, she had rediscovered. From the comfort of air conditioning, she could peer from the massive glass walls and see the river's termination, see the docking station where flocks of tourists waited to board the next river boat.

Though she wanted—no, needed—to get lost in a crowd, she could not take a chance on attracting attention, could not risk being remembered. She strolled every corridor of the busy mall. She had to keep going, but not over the same aisles. Someone might notice.

In her navy suit and pumps, she was out of place. Her first instinct had been to purchase casual clothes and *low-heeled* shoes. But she could not risk using her credit cards. Those who wanted her dead had vast resources with which to trace her.

Hell, she couldn't even use her cell phone for the exact same reason.

She exited the air conditioning and found herself walking along the *Paseo del Rio*. Ah! Another memory. The city's notable tourist attraction—other than the Alamo—was called the *Paseo del Rio*. River Walk.

Swinging her shoulder bag nonchalantly, she fell in step with the parade of those making their way along the *Paseo del Rio*. She was struck by how many uniformed young airmen she saw. Then another fact surfaced. Baby-faced teenagers, submitting themselves to head shaving and rigid inspections of their crisp blue uniforms, came from all over the country for basic training right here in San Antonio.

Before long, she found herself walking along the tree-shaded river bank, periodically looking over her shoulder to see if anyone were following her. Everything seemed normal, and she wandered into the midst of another swarm of busy pedestrians, most likely hurrying to dinner shared with loved ones. They seemed indifferent to the cobblestone paths and tropical foliage surrounding them at every turn.

Below the busy streets of the metropolis, the river cut its lazy bed through the towering city. And all along its generous path sprawled miniature jungles of tropical greenery and trees as strong and powerful as the river itself. Borders of red day lilies, orange and yellow zinnias, and pink, purple and white petunias colored the walk.

Lacy admired man's hand in this setting. The alternating limestone and pebbled walkways relieving the drab slabs of concrete blended well with nature's handiwork. Even the riverside restaurants did not detract from the charm. One sidewalk cafe had been built around a massive oak tree.

What Lacy liked most about the River Walk, especially now that she wanted to be lost in a safe crowd, was that it was designed for the masses to enjoy.

She looked behind her again. Two men in western shirts, hats, and boots followed. This was the second time she had noticed them. It seemed unlikely the two men were tourists. She wondered what they were doing on the

Paseo del Rio when she realized with sickening clarity they were following her. She told herself to stay calm, not to fall to pieces. Her safest course would be to stay where the most people were. They couldn't get her as long as there were this many witnesses.

Her brisk pace continued. She looked back only after each major bend of the river. The two men remained ten to fifteen feet behind her, careful not to stare.

She considered summoning one of the frequently passing river patrol boats for aid but discarded the idea because the authorities might also be seeking her. Either alternative could prove fatal. She could see the news headlines now: ...*shot while fleeing police.*

How long could she keep this up? A couple more hours, then what? She didn't have a weapon. And there was no one to whom she could turn. Her thoughts suddenly pivoted to Mike. He would know what to do. But she didn't want to endanger an innocent person.

Her only hope was eluding them, and her chances of doing that would be better after dark. She was hungry and her feet hurt, but she would have to keep walking until then.

In the murky waters of the San Antonio River meandering beside her, Lacy saw her own reflection. Trim figure, neat shoulder-length hair. If only she hadn't worn high heels that morning. She was starting to limp.

Strangely, she felt no pain. Only numbness. Lacy had experienced all the fear her system would tolerate in one day. Though her legs mechanically moved, she was weary. And almost ready to sit down on one of the riverside benches where she could be overtaken by the two. But from deep within, she pulled strength and kept up her pace, straining from time to time to catch pieces of the men's conversation. They spoke in hushed tones, their words strung together into mush she could not understand.

At the L-shaped curve of the river, Lacy saw a broad, concrete stairway she could take to the street twenty feet up. The stairs would carry her near the HemisFair Plaza, a vast remnant of the almost forgotten world's fair of 1968. She stepped on the second step and turned to look back in a casual manner. The two men were not there. She climbed to the top of the stairs and pivoted, coming back down again, her eyes sweeping over the dense flow of people, searching for the two men in western shirts.

They were nowhere to be seen.

Furious at herself for foolishly suspecting innocent passersby of following her, she knew she would have to find help or she would soon lose her sanity. Why did her thoughts keep riveting to Mike? She went back to the riverside again and walked past sidewalk restaurants and what would be gala night spots in a few hours when the blanket of darkness covered the city.

Eventually, she got off the River Walk and found herself in a section of downtown which had undoubtedly been prosperous several decades ago. But that was no longer the case. Now it was a refuge to those Spanish-speaking immigrants who had crossed the Rio Grande in search of a better life for their families.

With an unfamiliar flutter in her stomach, she thought once more of her former lover, Mike Talamino.

He was the finest man she had ever known. When he had come out of law school he had turned down a law firm job offering an annual salary of nearly a quarter of a million dollars. Fluent in Spanish, he had taken a modest-paying job with the Central Texas Legal Defense League where he could help Hispanics. He obtained divorces for abused young mothers and fought against corrupt landlords.

Then, Lacy thought with a little catch in her heart, he had moved to Houston to take a position as a civil rights attorney for the U.S. Department of Justice. It hurt too bad now to remember their breakup.

Everywhere she looked she saw brown people. She wondered what this land had looked like two centuries earlier when Spaniards had settled it, long before the

Anglos had come. Each snatch of conversation she heard now was in rapid Spanish. Signs written in Spanish beckoned from behind each storefront window. She smiled when she mentally translated one which read: *Zapatas* $9.99.

It was while she was smiling that she saw the policeman. She could hardly have missed seeing him because the sidewalks here were nearly empty. He headed toward her, his eyes never leaving hers. How could she escape him? He was fifty yards away. She continued walking toward him. Changing course might arouse suspicion.

His gaze swept past her, over her shoulder. Perhaps he wasn't after her. They couldn't know she was in San Antonio, she tried to assure herself. Still, she quivered inside and considered escape routes in the upcoming block. The store on the corner had entrances on both blocks. If necessary, she could run through it, coming out on the intersecting block.

She did not want to attract his attention, but as they drew near each other, she looked him in the eye.

He smiled. "Hi, ma'am."

She forced a smile and walked quickly past him, her body trembling uncontrollably.

She kept turning back, making certain he was not watching her. He never looked back.

Relief rushed over her. The policeman's

interest in her was no different than most men's. Her good looks never went unnoticed. She told herself she should be used to it. For her entire 25 years, she had been a noted beauty. But any man's interest baffled her today. She could not believe anyone could find her attractive after all she had endured and the miles she had traveled since she had donned her suit and applied her makeup at seven that morning in Austin.

Had that been the same day? Her mind quickly traced over the day's movements. Yes, she thought, it was on this same morning she had taken breakfast as usual. And she had dressed for work as usual. But nothing about the remainder of the day was routine. Her heart hammered as she recalled climbing out the bathroom window at the Sears.

What would have become of her if she had not been able to leave Austin and flee to San Antonio? She wondered by what method they had planned to kill her. She was by no means safe yet. Just because she had removed herself from the eye of the storm did not mean its devastating gales could not reach her.

Perhaps the most despairing aspect of her situation was that she had kept the dangerous secret to herself far too long. No one would believe her story. The FBI agent who was now dead had told her so two weeks earlier, and her story had not been as ridiculous as it was now. Others who might listen to her could be bought off.

She wondered again if there was anyone to whom she could turn. And again, she thought of Mike. It wouldn't be right to get him mixed up in this mess. Her mess. A mess he had instinctively warned her about. Oh, God, why hadn't she listened? Why hadn't she flown to Houston to repair their rift? Why had she let the love of her life get away?

Night crept up so slowly, she was startled when at last she noticed it.

As she paused to catch her breath, an ancient hotel—*not* one that had been refurbished in recent decades—caught her attention, and a force from within pulled her to it. She soon found herself in the lobby of the half-forgotten downtown hotel. It was a shabby old place with a skinny little lobby filled with derelicts sitting around on banged up benches and cheap vinyl couches. The badly worn carpet looked like something from a grand old movie house of a bygone era. She didn't know what had attracted her until she saw, almost hidden over in the corner, two mahogany phone booths.

She tossed a glance at the middle-aged man behind the desk. "Do the phones work?"

"They shore do, ma'am."

Her mouth curved into a smile as she strode to the first one. She sat on the interior stool, closed the door and lifted the receiver to place a telephone call to Mike Talamino in Houston.

Chapter 2

Until she placed the call, Lacy had not known she was going to call Mike. She had not seen him in nearly two years. But now that her life—as well as the lives of others—was in danger, he seemed the only one in the state who could help. If she was sure of anything, it was of Mike's complete honesty. No one could corrupt him.

After the second ring, she mumbled a plea. Three rings and still no answer. Surely he wouldn't have changed his cell number. He was her only chance. Four rings. He answered.

The warmth of his voice reassured her that calling him had been the right thing to do.

"Hello, Mike."

"Lacy?"

"Yes."

There was a silence, then he spoke. "Is it really you? God, I was just thinking about you today. I heard on the radio about you and Chambers." His voice was dry. Cool.

"I'm not going to marry him." Her voice shook. "Oh, Mike, I can't say much on the phone, but please believe me. I'm afraid I'm going to be killed. I've managed to escape, but I've got to have help---"

"Slow down. What's wrong?"

"I can't go into that now. Please don't tell anyone. It could be---"

"Where are you?"

"I'm in San Antonio." She paused. "Could you possibly come here?"

"Of course. I'll leave right now."

"Thank God." Her voice cracked. Tears spilled from her eyes. "How long will it take you?"

"It's a four-hour drive, but maybe I can get there sooner on a plane. Let me check the airlines and call you back."

The ensuing wait worried her. What if his phone was bugged? Or would someone be watching his house? Would they be watching the airports? If a five-minute wait was this hard on her, how could she manage a four-hour one?

He rang back after five minutes. "Listen, I'm on the way to the airport. I got a flight and can be in San Antonio in about two hours. Where do you want me to meet you?"

"How about the little Mexican restaurant on the river, *Casa del Rio*?" She had passed by it earlier in the evening and thought the name appropriate.

"I'll be there before ASAP."

"Mike . . ." She paused, remembering the

confiscated letter.

"Make absolutely certain no one follows you. There's a remote possibility you might be under surveillance."

"Me?"

"Possibly."

"Why?"

"I'll tell you all about it when you get here. Just please be careful."

"You too."

Her step seemed lighter as she set off for the Mexican restaurant. She had not eaten since breakfast, and that had been twelve hours ago.

If anything could be enjoyable after the harrowing events of the day, the Mexican food the little restaurant offered was. She ordered the Mexican platter: enchiladas, tacos, refried beans, Spanish rice and guacamole salad. Normally she would not have finished it, but she cleaned her plate and began snacking on chips.

The dozens of colorful umbrella tables scattered along the riverfront had caught her attention when she entered the restaurant, but her table was not on the water. She could be spotted too easily there. Instead, she had selected a table on the restaurant's veranda. It was a good thing. There was a lengthy line of people sipping cocktails while waiting for a riverfront table.

With her food gone and her apprehension

over the impending meeting quickly
mounting, she began to think about Mike.
Lacy knew Mike was close to asking her to
marry him when she joined the staff of
Lieutenant Governor Jim Chambers. Mike did
not like Chambers. She frequently broke
dates with Mike so she could work overtime
drafting speeches for the boss she adored.

She and Mike had argued over the
lieutenant governor constantly. "What amazes
me," Mike had said, "is that you can't see
through him. You believe Chambers cares
about people." She had defended her boss,
and the relationship between her and Mike
fizzled away, spat by spat. Finally, Mike's
position in Houston gave them a good excuse
to dispense with the pretense of harmony.

In the midst of her reverie, she saw him. He
stood at the side entrance to the cafe,
scanning over the tables until he saw her.
When their eyes met, her stomach nearly gave
away. Seeing him brought back feelings she
had forgotten she had for the lean, dark
lawyer. By other people's standards, he might
not be considered handsome. Tonight he
seemed unbelievably good looking, standing
slightly over six feet with long, lean trunk and
shoulders that were wide but not muscle
bound. His face was pensive with piercing
brown eyes framed with rimless glasses. He
had not smiled, but she could not help
remembering that crooked, almost sensuous

grin of his.

The dead-sexy smile did not seem to go with the rest of him. There was an almost OCD neatness about his appearance that coupled with an air of intelligence was wildly divergent from that devilish grin.

As she remembered his deep tenderness, she caught her breath. *What a fool I was.*

His face betrayed no emotion. He stalked across the floor to her table, his eyes sweeping over those who surrounded her. "Ready?"

She nodded, and with a grim face, rose, still queasy inside.

When they reached the street, he spoke. "I suppose you've a long story to tell."

She nodded and let him lead.

"Well, we'd better find a safe place. I don't think it's the kind of thing you talk about in the rear of a cab, is it?"

"No."

"You say you've been followed, but you managed to lose them?"

"Yes. In Austin. As far as I know, they don't know I'm here." She tried to sound casual. She wasn't quite ready to bare her fears to him. She would need a while to slip back to their former familiarity.

Right now she still felt adoring and awkward. "We're talking powerful people."

"Good grief, Lacy, why haven't you tried to disguise yourself? You know, you might be considered uncommonly beautiful."

They walked in silence, Lacy feeling feather light because he had said she was uncommonly beautiful. They entered a downtown variety store that was still open. It was one of those large stores that stocked everything from cosmetics to cheap dishes. Mike marched to the closest thing the store had to a men's clothing section, and he grabbed a straw hat.

Lacy would be hard pressed to say what kind of hat it was. It looked like something her grandfather wore fishing. Mike stuck it on her head. It was much too big.

"Got anything to pin up your hair with?" he asked.

She shook her head.

"What about a rubber band?"

She suddenly remembered she had in her purse some index cards with bits of research and topic ideas for future speeches. And around them was thick rubber band. She reached in her purse and removed the band from the cards. Then she swept back her dark hair and secured it with the rubber band.

Mike checked several hats for size until he found one marked small. "Try this," he said, smashing it on her head.

"Mike, I couldn't possibly---"

"You will," he commanded.

They walked down another aisle. He pointed at the eye makeup. "You better pick up some of this stuff, too. How about some of that purple eye goop and lots of that red junk for your cheeks?"

She wanted to protest but didn't dare. She was clearly in the subservient position now.

"You need to get out of that suit," he said, sorting through a pile of Alamo souvenir T-shirts. "Get one of these and some jeans. Sloppy, loose fitting jeans."

"You want to get men's?" she asked sarcastically.

"Not a bad idea." He led her to what passed for a clothing department and held up the smallest pair of men's pants, looked at her petite body, and said, "No way. We'd better get women's."

"I promise to get two sizes too big."

The first hint of his old smile returned.

She put cheap blue denim jeans and canvas tennis shoes in the basket which held the hat, T-shirt and makeup.

Before leaving the store, Mike selected still another guise, a pair of cheap reading glasses.

"I may end up with Barnum and Bailey yet," she said dryly.

His crooked grin reappeared.

The bond between them was still there. She was comforted by the thought.

After paying for the camouflaging devices, they trekked back to the River Center mall, where he selected an inexpensive overnight bag.

"What's that for?"

"Part of my plan."

"Oh, that explains a lot."

"You'll see."

They walked toward the cash register.

"Now," he said, "we need to find a place where you can put on your disguise without anyone seeing the transformation."

"No one would notice in this store. It's pretty busy. Why don't I find the women's restroom, put on the stuff and meet you outside?"

"Sounds good."

He slowly turned his head, his eyes sweeping across the floor of the store. "No one seems to be watching," he whispered. "Meet me where we came in."

He walked away.

She located the women's restroom easily, relieved that she did not have to make any inquiries. Calling attention to herself was the last thing she wanted to do. Especially since her picture was in the news today.

No one shared the restroom with her. She entered a stall and took off the navy suit, swapping for the sloppy T-shirt and sloppy jeans and stuffing what represented a week's salary into the plastic sack. Next, she left the stall, quickly applied the purple eye shadow and red blush under the harsh lights of the restroom's mirrors. Last, she plopped on the hat and put on the glasses. No way could she wear that hat. It was night, for crissake! She'd really call attention to herself if she walked around with the straw hat on. Mike had selected the lowest magnification number for the glasses so they would not be too different from normal vision.

They met at the assigned place and began to walk along the *Paseo del Rio* until they came to a tile-roofed Spanish looking hotel. Its rooms featured iron-railed balconies that overlooked the river. "We'll stay here," he said.

"That's why you wanted the suitcase."

He gave her a sly nod.

As soon as they got to their room, she sat on the sofa. She was so glad to sit down. There were blisters on her heels. Her gaze fanned over the spacious room. It featured French windows which led out to the balcony that overlooked the *Paseo del Rio*. Mike came to sit beside her and stretched his arm across her back, pulling her to him. Her heart fluttering, she scooted closer. He made her as lightheaded as champagne.

"I'm surprised you've restrained your laughter." She yanked off the reading glasses."What name did you use to check us in?" She'd told him not to use his real name.

"I thought I'd see if I could pass for Hispanic. How do you like Miguel Perez?"

"I actually have a cousin with that name. One of my three-hundred or so cousins."

He smiled again. "The door's locked. You're safe. Now tell me everything."

Chapter 3

"I suppose I'd better start at the beginning," Lacy said. "But, hell, where did it all begin?" She spoke more to herself than to him.

"Just take it easy and try to remember everything you can."

"Using your courtroom manner on me?" Her warm brown eyes met his pensive ones, and she felt compelled to go on with her story. . .

* * *

. . . It had all begun, she told Mike, on a typical work day only a couple of weeks before. She had come to work that morning, just as she did each day, turning her car on to the Capitol grounds. Dozens of tourists already speckled the well manicured grounds with overhanging trees and splashing bursts of flowers in neat parterre gardens.

Although she would never admit it, Lacy harbored a deep sense of pride each morning as she parked her modest car in one of the scarce parking slots on the Capitol grounds, knowing these reserved parking places were at a premium. She slanted her car into its space and walked the few short steps to the door of the magnificent structure.

The massiveness of the building's interior always awed her. It was larger than Parliament and more imposing. Fifteen thousand train carloads of Texas red granite had gone into its construction. An army regiment could pass through the vast hallways. Each hand-carved doorway reached to heights of eighteen feet. Lacy could never walk through these halls without thinking of what a bitter, liberal state legislator had said of the building before she was ever born. "This building was built for giants and is inhabited by Pygmies."

Lacy thought of her boss. *Maybe our giant has arrived.*

She was relieved her correspondence was out of the way. She could spend the day on the speech the lieutenant governor was to deliver the following day to a group of educators in Dallas. Jim wanted to target early childhood. Since improving the state's day care programs was something she cared deeply about, she hoped to come up with a unique speech on the subject—not just the usual enumeration of current programs and professional recommendations.

When she entered the outer chamber to her office she heard Suzanne, the secretary she shared with the lieutenant governor's itinerary secretary, say, "Oh, just a minute,

Miss Blair's just come in."

Suzanne put her hand over the receiver. "Someone from the lieutenant governor's campaign office wants to talk to you."

"I'll take it in my office," Lacy called over her shoulder.

The caller turned out to be Phil Goodson, the lieutenant governor's gubernatorial campaign chairman.

"I wanted to talk to you, Lacy, about that day care speech you're doing. Richard and I think it will give Jim a good opportunity to come out loudly for some new programs. And that may just help swing a few more votes his way."

"You know I want to see Jim in the governor's mansion as much as anyone, but as a state employee, I'm not permitted to direct my nine-to-five hours toward that pursuit."

"Where do you draw the line between a candidate's campaign promises and a lieutenant governor's statement on possible legislation?"

"I wish I knew."

"I'm not trying to twist your arm. I'm only asking that you do some research and make some noble, innovative proposals for Jim to recommend."

"I would be happy to do that."

"You might want to talk to Raymond Hawn over at the welfare office."

"Okay, Phil."

"Try to work up a rough draft for me today."

She had barely hung up when the intercom came on.

"Lacy, Richard said he wanted to see you as soon as you came in."

"Thanks, Suz."

Richard McNally was the one person Lacy could not keep waiting. She set off immediately for his office, which was next to the lieutenant governor's. He had been Jim's top aide since the time Jim tossed his hat in the statewide political arena. His duties ranged from working the Senate floor during a legislative session to sending telegrams of condolence in the name of the lieutenant governor. He did all the hiring and firing for the Senate, and he was the man who gave Lacy orders.

Richard's office reflected his wife's impeccable taste. Rich deep pile in pale gold covered the floors. A living tree with healthy green leaves stood in one corner of the room. Handsomely framed historic documents hung on the longest wall while a recent photograph of the Capitol at night occupied the greater part of the skimpiest wall. His most prized possession, she knew, was his photo of George W. Bush with an inscription to Richard, a fellow Texan. The rugged roll-top desk Richard sat at was equally impressive.

Vivian McNally's scavenging in the Capitol's basement had turned it up, and the craftsman she hired restored it to look as it had when a turn-of-the-century governor had used it.

Richard was locking his file cabinet when Lacy entered. He put the key in his top desk drawer and locked it. Lacy had always wondered about that file cabinet. She supposed it contained data on important contributors.

Lacy wondered how old Richard was. His receding hairline was deceiving. He could be anywhere between thirty-five and fifty. His sandy-colored hair showed no gray, but a patch of crow's feet surrounded his bright green eyes. Those could be caused just as much by hard work as by age, she thought, just as his chalky skin was due to his constant work indoors more than to heredity. If he lost ten pound he would look younger, she decided. He wasn't fat, just thick around the waist.

"How are you today, Lacy?" He settled in his big oak swivel chair.

"I'd be fine if it weren't for so many interruptions. What do you guys have against letting a girl do her work?"

"What I want to talk to you about won't take a minute. Jim's still barnstorming up in the Panhandle and won't be in 'till late this afternoon when he's scheduled to make an appearance at the high school convention meeting here. He wants you to be his date tonight at the Headliners party, but the problem is his schedule won't allow him to pick you up—nothing new I know. But, he did want me to make sure you didn't mind meeting him there."

"Of course not." Jim was always so thoughtful, she thought with affection.

"Good. And I don't suppose I need to tell you to remain mute on the snooping reporters' questions about wedding bells, do I?"

"It galls me they bring up a subject like that when his wife hasn't been dead a year."

"I know. If only they had seen his grief firsthand as we did. But he's doing much better now—with your help. I wouldn't be surprised if you aren't the next first lady of Texas."

"You're embarrassing me. Really, there's been nothing between us." She rose. "I hope I don't see you again until tonight. I'll be out of my office this morning researching that day care speech."

Back in her office, she could not help thinking about what Richard had said. She had thought Jim Chambers' partiality toward her was out of professional respect. When she joined his staff he took a great deal of time with her, teaching her his particular style of speech-making along with his goals, both legislative and political.

Now she rarely had to consult him before drafting a speech. She knew when to use chronological order. She knew when pathos or humor could be used effectively. She knew how to please him as well as the Texans who had set him up as a demigod.

Now that she thought about it, there had been romantic gestures on Jim's part. He was never too busy to think of her feelings. And whenever he was out of town he called her on the pretext of discussing a speech. On her birthday he had treated the staff to a lunch at her favorite restaurant, a Mexican one in the *barrio* of East Austin, and he had sent her a dozen yellow roses, saying she was his "Yellow Rose of Texas."

Until today, she had never admitted a romance could be possible between Jim Chambers and her. She pushed those thoughts out of her mind. Lacy had dismissed any gestures he made toward her. Especially when his wife had been alive. After all, he's a politician, she told herself. It's his job to make each person feel special, each agenda important.

What about the time, she now wondered, when she first started working for Jim and he called her into his office and asked her to stand beside him as he looked out over the tree tops of the Capitol grounds. He had put his arm around her and spoke solemnly. "We can rule this land, make it a better place."

Feeling uncomfortable with his arm around her, she watched him as his gaze fell on the Governor's Mansion across the street. "What we're going to do is bigger than Texas," he had said. Why had she felt the *we* was not the politician's verbal rhetoric? Had he meant *we* as in him and me? she wondered. But what about his wife?

The frumpy Mrs. Chambers was no longer an obstacle. She was dead.

Chapter 4

Scanning through her files on day care programs was of little help in composing the speech, but the day care section of the appropriations bill gave Lacy an idea. Five million dollars had been allocated for establishment of a day care center serving children of migrant farm workers. The federal government had matched the state's money, each of them providing two and a half million. The program was being initiated in Schneiderburg, Jim's old senatorial district.

Since Schneiderburg was less than a two-hour drive away, Lacy decided to drive there and talk to the program director and the children. She could take slides for a slide presentation.

Schneiderburg was the county seat of Schneiderburg County. The population of the entire county was not as large as that of most county seats. Most or its residents were white, but several hundred migrant farm workers made their home there during harvesting season.

If the city was famous for citrus fruit, it

was even more famous for giving the state Jim Chambers. And giving the state Jim Chambers had given Schneiderburg several distinctions, one of them being the modern highway upon which Lacy was now driving. On the outskirts of the downtown area Lacy noticed a small shopping center built in the Spanish style with tiled roof and a multi-arched colonnade. It was called Hacienda Square. From its name she guessed the shops must all face a central courtyard like a Mexican hacienda. She wondered if the center was air conditioned.

Further down the highway Lacy came to the old town square constructed of German-inspired masonry popular in the late eighteen-hundreds. Fashioned like most Southern county seats, the courthouse served as the square around which the old town was built. Lacy noticed a surprising number of fine antique shops, dress shops, along with a shoe shop, a drug store, a movie house and a café with a scattering of hanging baskets and outdoor tables—all of which were filled.

Since it was nearly noon, she decided to sample the luncheon fare at the cafe. Though the café's exterior looked trendy, the narrow interior was pure vintage. Everything here, from the square chrome-legged tables to the asphalt tile and neon lights overhead, was utilitarian.

Not wanting to take up a whole table

during this obviously busy lunch period, she took the only available seat at the end of the counter.

A young Hispanic girl sporting a polo shirt with the cafe's logo cleared away the dirty dishes in front of Lacy and wiped off the counter as a well groomed blonde with long, fake fingernails and a proprietary air tended the cash register next to Lacy.

In a deep Southern drawl, she explained they were shorthanded because a waitress had quit the day before. Lacy finally gave her order to a young waitress then asked if she could direct her to the state's day care center.

A blank look crossed the waitress's face. "Never heard of it," she said.

A middle-aged man sitting next to Lacy spoke up. "If it's the building you're lookin' for, you'll find it about three miles down Sheridan Highway, but you won't find nothin' there. The program ain't actually started yet. Don't reckon it ever will. Folks around here don't go for spending their tax money on them Mexicans--"

"Excuse me," Lacy interrupted, "you must be mistaken. I know a center has been initiated in this town. I'm here from the capital, and money most certainly was earmarked for that purpose."

"Well, there's been talk of getting one, and that old church was bought--"

"Excuse me, honey, but I heard you say

you were from the capital," the well-groomed blonde said to Lacy. "Do you know our Jim Chambers?"

"I work for him," Lacy said with pride.

"Well, isn't that something, Cecil?"

"Been going to the first Baptist Church with Jim since he was knee high to a grasshopper," Cecil said.

"Finest boy that ever lived. That's what I always tell them reporters that come here to write up about Jim. I was quoted in *Texas Monthly* magazine, you know," the blonde said proudly. "Tell me, honey, does Jim know you're here?"

"No. I'm doing research on day care centers. The lieutenant governor is giving a speech on child care programs tomorrow, and I write his speeches."

"Ain't that nice," the woman said. The almost-too-friendly smile left her face and she spoke somberly. "Honey, I'm sorry your trip was for nothing, but we don't have that nursery school yet. Expect it real soon, though. You should have checked with Jim before you came. He'd have told you about it." She turned her attention to a customer approaching the cash register.

Lacy didn't like the food. Maybe it wasn't the food. Maybe it was the sick feeling she had for having wasted her day and making a fool of herself. Why hadn't she checked with someone before she came?

She had, though, checked the last appropriations bill. Two-and-a-half million dollars for purchase of a suitable structure, furnishings and teaching supplies. Her knowledge of state appropriations convinced her the money had to be used during the current biennium, and the biennium was nearly over. She had been under the impression that a fairly large site had been purchased. Perhaps she bad better go see the building on Sheridan Highway.

As Lacy slid into the front seat of her car she saw a body crouched on the floor. She gasped, her heart drumming wildly, her hand groping for the door handle. She started to scream, then recognized the intruder as the Hispanic girl who had cleaned off the counter.

The young girl pressed her index finger to her lips. "Please, no one must know I talk to you. I be finished after lunch in about one hour. I must talk to you. Meet me on the other side of the bridge back where the trees are. Don't let anyone see you. I go now." She poked her head barely above the seat, looked in every direction, opened the door and briskly walked around the corner toward the rear of the cafe.

Lacy was left shaken. What did the girl want to tell her? Could it have something to do with the day care center?

She drove down Sheridan Highway. The three miles over which she drove revealed exactly two dwellings. One was an abandoned shack with a sagging front porch and glassless windows; the other was a small farm house. The third structure on the little-traveled road was the old church Lacy sought. It had once been a church, Lacy guessed by the steeple and wide front steps and doorway. It was typical of many rural Southern churches: a large white frame box. Fresh paint proclaimed it to be "PROPERTY OF THE STATE OF TEXAS." A padlock secured the door.

There was nothing more to see.

As she drove through town again to reach the bridge, Lacy periodically checked her rear-view mirror to be certain no one was following her. When she was certain, she turned her car into a densely wooded field close to the bridge. She drove the car downward toward a ravine which emptied into the river. The gentle slope hid her car from the road. She looked around again and saw no one. She looked at her watch. Fifteen more minutes. She was nervous and scared and did not know why. What was there for her to fear?

There had been fear in the girl's face.

Even the forest of trees couldn't protect Lacy from the sweltering heat. She was hot and sticky and scared. She wished she had not come. Her cold office with its cold floors and metal desk would be a welcome retreat now.

Before long, she heard a sudden noise. It sounded as if twigs were cracking beneath someone's steps. Queasiness filled her stomach, then she saw it was the Hispanic girl.

Although her walk was nearly brisk enough for a run, the young girl examined the path she trod closely and chose her steps carefully. Lacy judged her to be around sixteen. In addition to the café's shirt, she wore jeans and athletic shoes. A sensible choice for one who had to work on her feet all day. It bothered Lacy that such a young girl had to work all day.

"I thought maybe you would not come," she told Lacy.

As she had done before, the girl looked in each direction. Lacy suggested they sit in her car. As they walked to the car, the girl said she had taken a chance on the red Toyota being Lacy's because of the parking sticker from the Capitol.

They got in the car.

"I won't take long. First, you must never say you have talked to me," the girl said. "It could be very dangerous for me. The Anglos don't like us. That is why I have to talk to you. The lady with the hair of yellow, my boss, she doesn't know I speak English. She say many things I think she would not like me to hear. There was to be a nursery school for our children when their mamas are working in the fields. This we wanted very much. But we will never have it. Mr. Chambers and the people of the town fixed it so."

Lacy attempted a protest at hearing her boss slandered, but the young girl cut in sharply.

"It is so. I heard my boss talking with the town's realtor. They used the money for the school to build the new shopping center, Hacienda Square. On paper they made it look like they paid the whole amount for the Sheridan Highway property and building."

"You can't be serious!"

The girl nodded. "I tell you these things, but I will tell no one else. I do not fear for myself but for my parents and my brothers and sisters. I hoped you could help us, but now I fear for you. My boss tried to call Mr. Chambers after you left. She couldn't get him, but she talked to Mr. Mac something. I didn't hear what else she say. She talked in a whisper, but you could be in trouble."

"This is all so unbelievable. I've known Jim Chambers for two years. He's been a good legislator," Lacy defended.

"Believe it. Mr. Chambers is evil. He is like those mafia men in the movies who have people killed. You mustn't go back to him. You are now in danger."

"That's ridiculous. Jim Chambers couldn't hurt a fly." Lacy stopped for a minute, then asked, "Give me one shred of evidence, and I'd help you—to prove him right, if for no other reason."

The girl got out of the car. "Please believe these things. I have no proof. I only know that what I say is true."

Chapter 5

Part of the aura which had attracted Lacy to a political life had been the gala Washington parties she read about. The women in their haute couture, the sprinkling of cosmopolitan ambassadors, the debates over tomorrow's laws. They all added to that magical lure Lacy had found so enticing.

The Austin political get-togethers supplied no such glamour. Tonight's affair called for somewhat dressy attire. Lacy chose a white linen suit with matching heels. She examined herself in the mirror and approved of the attractive reflection.

"Well, you couldn't be any straighter if you had a two by four down your spine," Becky, Lacy's roommate, teased. "What is it tonight?"

"A reception for lawmakers. The Headliners are hosting it."

"Wow," Becky mocked, "And I bet you get to stand in one of these boring receiving lines pretending to be delighted over the never-ending stream of people you don't know."

Lacy laughed.

"Going with Smiling Jim?"

"Yep," Lacy nearly whispered. She was thinking again of what the girl had told her that day about Jim. She knew she had to handle the time bomb of suspicions with all the shrewdness and aloof coolness she could muster. She had thought it strange that afternoon that McNally hadn't contacted her when she returned from Schneiderburg. She had been in her office all afternoon throwing together a promissory speech on improving Texas day care.

Goodson scanned it and told her it was precisely what he had in mind. But still she had not heard from McNally. Because of what the girl had said, Lacy knew he had heard of her jaunt to Schneiderburg. He must have decided to approach the subject casually at tonight's party. She decided to wait for McNally to make the first move.

* * *

Lacy impatiently eyed the hands on her watch and the elevator dial at the same time. She'd had some difficulty finding a parking place. If she wasn't at the club on the top floor of the high-rise hotel in four minutes, she would be late. When one had to stand in a receiving line, one simply wasn't late. She kept pressing the UP button, although she knew one push was enough. She was about to push again when a man's voice chided her.

"On your way to a fire?"

She turned around and greeted Jim

Chambers.

He stood looking down at her from his six-foot-two inch height. His presence was commanding, his manner confident. It helped that he was young—thirty-two—and possessed blond good looks. "Don't worry. We're not late," he said. "Even if we were, they can't start without me." He smiled down at her. She suddenly felt awkward.

They rode the elevator alone. Jim pressed against Lacy and firmly secured her hand in his much larger one.

"I won't be able to do this the rest of the evening," he whispered. His dark eyes longingly raked over her. "You're beautiful."

She cast her eyes downward. Her lashes nearly rested on her cheeks. "Thank you, Jim."

As the elevator came to a halt on the top floor, Jim dropped her hand and straightened his tie before making his entrance.

The boisterous crowd hushed when they entered. All eyes shifted to the handsome couple. Although Lacy moved gracefully and retained a soft smile, she shook inwardly. She never had become accustomed to being a focal point.

Becky had been right about the receiving line, Lacy thought. In her first thirty minutes there she had not talked to more than a dozen people she knew. Among those had been the McNallys. As cordial as ever,

McNally did not mention her morning excursion.

Lacy and Jim were greeting the last couple in line when a lone youngish male approached. Jim was deep in conversation with a couple, so Lacy offered her hand to the newcomer and introduced herself.

"Jeff Holcomb." His firm hand gripped hers.

"Are you from Austin, Jeff?" She had mastered techniques of engaging strangers in conversation.

"No, I'm with Judge Taylor in Houston."

Lacy knew Judge Taylor was a federal district judge whom her old boyfriend, Mike Talamino, had been close to. "Oh, perhaps you know Mike Talamino."

"Why, yes. We're well acquainted. You must have known him when he was here in Austin."

Lacy nodded. "We *used* to be well acquainted." Why did the mention of Mike Talamino cause her heart to flutter and her knees to feel weak? She had a sudden hunger to see him. Her dark, bespectacled knight. God, she didn't realize how badly she had missed him. "How is he?"

"Working himself to death, as usual. Never relaxes. It would probably take five men to replace him."

"Sounds as if he hasn't time for play," Lacy said. "Which makes me wonder if he has ever married." Her stomach plummeted at the thought of Mike marrying.

"Mike? You must be kidding. He's always so busy, traveling and so forth, that he's too busy to make it to any events which could be construed as social."

Noticing the couple Chambers had been talking to leave, Lacy said, "Well, Jeff, I hope you'll mention me to Mike. I'm glad I got to talk to you, but I'm sure you'd rather talk to Mr. Chambers than to me."

She went directly to the McNallys. "Vivian, you look pretty tonight. I think your new hairdo very becoming." Vivian McNally was a good-looking women in her late thirties.

"Oh, thank you, Lacy, but I must admit I haven't felt so pretty since I saw how gorgeous you look."

Lacy liked her a lot. She liked Lacy, too. Vivian liked everyone her husband respected. In fact, Lacy thought, her ideas were mere copies of her husband's, so enamored of him was she.

McNally joined the conversation. "I don't know how you do it, Lacy. Working like a programmed computer all day. I know you couldn't have finished before six o'clock. What I want to know is how you got home, dressed so nicely, ate and got back here by seven-thirty."

"Well, first of all, I didn't eat. And I'm famished. Why don't we go see what the Headliners have furnished us with in the way of hors d'oeuvres?"

"We skip a meal, then proceed to more than make up for calories by hitting the snack table at these affairs," Vivian said as she sauntered to the central table with her husband and Lacy.

Vivian was right about the calories. No fat-free delights were to be counted among the corn chips, jalapeno bean dip, jalapeno cheese dip and miniature fried chicken legs.

Sebastian, the roving waiter who served at most of these functions, not only knew Lacy by name but also remembered what she drank. After taking orders from the small crowd gathered around the snack table, he approached Lacy. "The usual, Miss Blair?"

"Yes, thank you, Sebastian," Lacy answered with a smile and a wink, for the usual for Lacy was plain Coke. It wasn't that she didn't like to drink, but that bartenders at these affairs mixed cocktails far too strong for Lacy to swallow comfortably. Hosts at these parties didn't quibble over a few more dollars spent on liquor as a night club manager might.

Besides Lacy and the McNallys, two former colleagues of Lacy's from the *News* and her former boss hovered over the long snack table. They struck up a conversation, then Jim joined them, slipping his arm around Lacy's shoulder.

The hum of private conversations ceased the instant Jim arrived at the table.

As if to break the edgy silence, Lacy's former boss at the *News* spoke. "Mr. Chambers, how many other state officials, besides yourself, have filed complete financial statements in the Secretary of State's office?"

"Well, in the way of a little campaigning, let me say I'm pleased to report nearly every candidate for a statewide office has now filed. Of course there are a few exceptions—one of my opponents in the upcoming primary among them. But I can't tell you how pleased I am that so many have followed my lead."

"Sounds smart," the editor said. "I'm pleased to inform you that my paper is considering two editorials which I think will give you a great deal of satisfaction. First, we're going to back your candidacy for the governorship, and second we're going to demand—editorially, of course—enactment of the tax break legislation you've been proposing."

"I can't tell you how pleased I am," Chambers proudly announced. "I can tell you that if elected I will serve the people of Texas with dignity and leadership—those two adjectives originally furnished by my speech writer here." He indicated Lacy.

"Yes, Governor, one of the wisest choices you ever made was taking her away from us. I was pretty mad at you at the time." Turning to Lacy, he said, "You know, Lacy, if you had stayed at the *News* you could have written your own ticket, probably could have been the paper's first woman editor. But, who knows, you may attain a higher honor." His gaze flicked from her to Jim.

Lacy brushed off that romantic innuendo and the dozen or so others that followed during the evening.

No matter where she and Chambers wandered in the room, they always ended up in a comfortable group which included the McNallys. McNally chose his moment carefully. When Jim mentioned his trip to Dallas on the following morning, McNally said, "Speaking of Jim's trip, Lacy, how did that day care speech go? I was swamped this afternoon and didn't get a chance to check with you about it."

Lacy forced a smile. "You wouldn't believe what a hectic time I had with that thing. Stupid me. I thought that pilot program in Schneiderburg had already been launched, so there I went, in all my honest stupidity, all the way to Schneiderburg—only to find out I was premature. So I wasted the entire morning and had to work frantically all afternoon on the speech. Mr. Goodson liked it, though."

"Well, that's good," McNally said as he glanced seriously at Jim.

"How'd you like my home town?" Jim asked.

"I'm sure I didn't see that much of it. It

didn't take too long to find out my trip was in vain. By the way, the lady who told me the day care center hasn't started yet told me to give you her regards. The blonde who I assume owns the café."

He nodded. "Dee Hesse. Known her all my life."

"I found Schneiderburg lovely. I was struck by the architectural blends. They symbolize, I think, the ethnic makeup of the town. You know, the old town of German masonry and lines representing the old—probably a German settlement at the turn of the twentieth century. And the stucco Spanish-type shopping center representing the turn of the twenty-first century.

The *News*' editor and the editor of the *Houston Chronicle* joined their group, asking Jim his opinion on the candidates running for the office he now held.

"I'm not going to endorse anyone before the primary. I will, of course, back the nominee of our party before the general election next November. Let me outline, however, the qualifications I think a candidate for this office should have. He should have previously held elected office. He should have strong leadership capabilities, and he should—and I want to stress this above all else—he should have integrity."

"Well put, Governor," Lacy's former editor said.

They speculated on how the primary vote would come out in the lieutenant governor's race and talked for a few minutes before Jim broke it up: "I could stay here with you all night, but I need to be politicking now. And, Thomas," Jim said to the *News'* editor, "any time you need me, remember my door is always open."

It was easy to see why he was so popular, thought Lacy.

Lacy and Jim dutifully circulated the room, finding something to say to each small group they encountered. Lacy had been told she was as popular as Jim, and people were already calling them the golden couple.

By custom, the governor was to leave these parties first, followed by the lieutenant governor. The governor left at nine fifteen. Lacy and Jim left at nine forty-five. Jim suggested following her home, telling her he worried about her driving alone through the dark hills and winding roads.

When they reached Lacy's house, she asked him in for a drink.

Chapter 6

Lacy balanced Scotch and water in her right hand, a chardonnay in her left. "I hope you like my weak drinks after those at the party. She set the drinks on the coffee table in front of the sofa where Jim sat.

"I like everything you do," he said softly.

She sat next to him.

The tranquil view of scattered lights from the sleeping city below stole his attention. "You've got it made here," he said. His eyes scanned the cozy room with its deeply tufted area rug over wood floors and a slip-covered sofa facing a bay window which overlooked the town. "I think I could sit here all night."

"What would my neighbors say? With those special license plates of yours, you must be very cautious."

"I'm considering swapping cars with Richard for nights like this."

He scooted closer to her and wrapped his arms around her as his lips claimed hers. It was their first kiss. They were almost never alone, and when they were he had always treated Lacy with such respect she wondered if he thought she were a piece or delicate porcelain which might crush from his touch.

But now that he had tenderly kissed her, Lacy's disappointment set in. No bells. No gosh-I-wish-this-minute-would-last-forever or anything. And all the while visions of Mike Talamino obliterated everything. Even though she hadn't seen Mike in almost two years, she vividly remembered the surge of liquid heat his touch evoked. Her uneasiness with Jim gave way to anger when his hand started fumbling with the zipper on the back of her skirt.

She pulled away, grasping his arms. "Jim, please don't spoil things."

"Lacy, Lacy Love, I am sorry. It's just that I've been waiting for this moment so long, I couldn't restrain myself. I've been in love with you since I first met you at that press conference."

Her mouth gaped open. "But you were married!"

"Not truly. Ruth and I hadn't lived as man and wife for years." He sighed. "Now that she's gone, I can declare my feelings toward you. I want you more than I've ever wanted anything. I want to marry you." His voice softened and he clasped her hand in his. "Please consider it."

Underlying what should have been the happiest moment of her life were the irksome accusations made by the Hispanic girl earlier in the day. If any part of the girl's story were true, Lacy knew she couldn't be his wife. She desperately wanted to disprove the allegations.

"If you're to marry me, I want you to know beforehand I'm no saint. To be honest, Ruth's death caused me no great anguish."

"But, Jim, I saw you at the funeral, and those weeks that followed you were too upset even to stay in Austin and perform your duties. I know you were grieving."

"Of course I felt bad, especially since I'd been considering asking Ruth for a divorce." He ran his hand through his curly blond hair. "Ruth and I were married before we were twenty years old. I simply outgrew her. Her petite size was a plus factor when she was a teenager and I was the basketball star at Schneiderburg High. Everyone said we were a cute couple. But when she was thirty and five-by-five it was no longer cute. Then, too, I graduated from college, and she never did. What misery it was being married to a woman I didn't love! Maybe if we'd had children...But, anyway, once I saw you I knew I had to have you."

If he thought his words should make her happy, he was gravely mistaken. She felt soiled, almost as if she had actually committed adultery—something Lacy would never do.

She stiffened.

Seeing that Lacy was not responding, he got up and walked around the living room. "Guess I've thrown too much at you too soon."

Lacy watched his craggy face. He looked tired. Tonight he looked older than his thirty-two years. She nodded.

He came back, dropped to one knee in front of her, and took her hand. "I'll give you more time." He looked at his watch. "Guess I'll head home. Got to leave early tomorrow for Dallas."

After he left, Lacy went to bed, but both the mystery novel she tried to read and her sleep were disturbed by thoughts of Jim Chambers. She was more confused than ever. One minute he could be a saint, the next a villain. What had troubled her most about him was his attitude toward his wife. How could he treat her death so callously? It was so out of character for him.

But what was his real character? True, he had always been more than considerate toward her, but it was obvious now that he wanted to impress her.

What about the Hispanic girl's accusations? She remembered, too, what Mike had once said about the uncanny hold Jim Chambers seemed to have over the Senate. *They fear him,* Mike had said.

Perhaps Jim Chambers wasn't the demigod she had thought. For the second time that night, she saw Mike in her mind's eye. She saw the dark stubble that covered his lean cheeks after a day's work. She saw his tie loosened, a look of concern etched across his pensive face. And suddenly she knew she could never marry Jim Chambers.

But that did not mean she could not try to exonerate him of evil-doing.

One thing she knew for certain. She would believe him innocent until she personally could prove otherwise. But how could she get at the truth? Jim had close allies in every part of the state. And she was quickly becoming well known as Jim Chambers' girl. Too many people could recognize her. She couldn't turn to anyone. The local district attorney and the state attorney general were both close to Jim.

Then she thought of someone who could help.

Chapter 7

Lacy never took over an hour for lunch, and today she had already spent twenty minutes of the lunch hour finding a place to park on the overcrowded university campus. She only hoped no one at the Capitol would miss her. She was going to be very late.

She had been instructed to wear a white ribbon in her hair and to select an orange book. She was to go to one of the unoccupied, glass-enclosed study rooms on the second floor of the undergraduate library. She was to take a seat with her back to the glass wall. Her contact was supposed to approach her and say, "Don't study too hard. It's not good for one."

She was thankful she did not have a lengthy wait. They had obviously been watching her since she stepped off the elevator. Two tallish men entered the cubical shortly after Lacy. The younger of the two sat across from her but several feet down. The older sat next to her and recited to her his pass phrase as he opened a loose-leaf notebook. A neatly taped plastic-coated card was centered on one of the pages of the notebook. It identified him as Joseph Bryson, an FBI special agent. The muscular agent was perhaps forty years old with thick blondish hair and had faded freckles across his puffy face.

"I don't need to know your name at this time, if you fear you might be in danger," he whispered. "I don't think you're being followed."

"No, I don't believe I'm in danger. Are you the man I talked to on the phone this morning?"

He nodded, then looked across the table at his partner. The younger agent didn't catch his glance. His eyes continuously scanned the outer room.

"Now, I think you better tell me your story," Bryson said. Like he did, she whispered. "I don't even know if anything's wrong, but it's just too risky, and I'm too well known around the Capitol to investigate this situation by myself. I don't mind telling you my name is Lacy Blair, I'm a speechwriter for the lieutenant governor. He's the person I want investigated."

At this, the agent raised his brows.

"I don't know anything for sure," she continued, "but I have suspicions that he may be involved in some illegal matters."

Lacy related the details of the trip to Schneiderburg. He wrote several notations in his notebook as she talked. She tried to read snatches of what he was writing but was not familiar with his peculiar shorthand. He did not interrupt her narrative, but when she finished asked several questions.

"First of all, you say the young girl will not tell anyone else her story?"

"As I told you, she said she's too scared. She didn't think anyone in Schneiderburg would talk."

"What's that Schneiderburg real estate man's name?"

"I don't remember her saying."

He frowned and shook his head. "By the way, how long have you worked for Chambers?"

"Two years."

"And in that time has he ever done anything that seemed suspicious?"

"Never."

He nodded.

"No wait..." She added, "That is, I never suspected him of doing anything underhanded, but since I went to Schneiderburg I seem to notice little things I never thought about before."

"Like what?"

"Like the almost magical hold he has over the Senate. I'm not saying he blackmails people or anything like that, but if he's capable of the other, then I think he's capable of doing that too. And I know this sounds silly, but I really started suspecting he wasn't the all-American boy next door when he told me last night that he wasn't upset by his wife's death."

"Didn't his wife die in an auto accident? Brakes failed on Mount Bonnel Road? That might be worth looking in to, too."

Lacy was stunned. She had never considered the possibility of Ruth Chambers having been murdered.

"Oh, no! Jim wouldn't have done that."

"In my job we must consider every possibility."

"I could never believe that. I know Jim Chambers would never hurt anyone. She shook her head. "Oh, I don't know why I'm doing this to him. I'm sorry I ever called you. I don't know what to think, so how can I expect you to?"

"Ma'am, because of Mr. Chambers' friends in high places, we may not be able to very calmly and hush-hush like investigate these charges, either. Our department has a public image to uphold. We don't go around making innuendos and accusations against well-liked public officials. I'll have to talk this over with our agent in charge."

He reached into his pocket, withdrawing a business card. A phone number, nothing else, was centered on the white rectangle.

"Here." He handed it to her. "Call me at this number, from a phone booth, at six o'clock tomorrow evening."

A phone booth? Surely her phones couldn't be bugged! She took the card and agreed to call at the appointed time. "You leave now. We'll follow in about ten minutes."

Lacy smiled and stood up. As she left the cubicle, she smiled at the other agent, the one who had not been close enough to listen.

* * *

The following day was so routine and Schneiderburg so far removed from the serenity of the spring day that Lacy forgot about calling the agent named Bryson. That is, until she was nearly home. She looked at her watch. It was five forty-five. She pulled the car into a drive-in grocery a couple of blocks from her house. There was no pay phone. She turned back toward town, knowing that finding a pay phone would be no easy task. She thought her luck might be better in one of the older hotels.

In downtown, she drove into the parking garage of one of the Austin's oldest hotels and parked. Just off the hotel's lobby, she found a row of phones. No privacy, but it wasn't likely, in this age of cell phones, that anyone would be using one of the other phones.

She was glad it actually worked. She dialed Bryson, then looked at her watch. Six-o-five.

Bryson answered promptly, his voice a harsh whisper as he told her he couldn't talk at that time, but he would meet her later that evening.

She agreed, and they decided to meet on the last row of a theater by the university. He made her promise to make certain no one was following her.

* * *

A girlish giggle cut through the silence inside Lacy's car that night as she drove to the movie and her meeting with Bryson. The giggle was hers; she hadn't been able to stifle it. Here she was dressed in bland khaki pants and shirt, dressing so that no one would notice her. She cautiously checked her rear-view mirror, making certain no one was following. All the cloak-and-dagger trappings of a prime suspense thriller were there—except there were no bad guys, no suspense, and no thrill. She laughed at how foolish she seemed, even to herself. She almost hadn't come, but she felt it was only fair to Bryson to tell him herself that she had been totally misdirected in her accusations toward Jim.

At the show, she spotted Bryson immediately. He sat alone in the middle of the theater's back row. There weren't more than twenty-five people in the theater, and most of them sat closer to the front. She and Bryson would be quite alone, she thought. No one could possibly overhear them. Besides, the small audience was already worked up to a state of hilarity over the comedy on the towering screen.

She quietly sat down next to Bryson.

"Do you think you'll be able to understand me over all this noise?" he asked.

She had not had any difficulty understanding the question. "No problem."

"Good. Now, Miss Blair, I'll have to be one hundred percent frank with you and explain that our department cannot investigate your charges. Do you have any idea what kind of a tornado we'd stir up in this state if we went around accusing its number two citizen of these actions? The FBI cannot be put in the position of impugning a political figure. It would be too easy for a political foe to try to manipulate the system."

"Of course I understand only too well. That's why I couldn't do it myself and asked you fellows in on---"

He interrupted. "There is the fact the federal government matched funds totaling two-and-a-half million. That makes it a federal case. The problem is Jim Chambers has friends in very high places. It would be virtually impossible to investigate him without him becoming aware of it."

Lacy nodded. "I perfectly agree with you, Mr. Bryson. I now feel that I was playing at my own urge to be a crusader against evil. I'm sure I must have been wrong. It can't be Jim. Schneiderburg and the Hispanic girl seem now like a dream, far removed. I can't believe I was actually there." Then her brows furrowed, and she shook her head. "But I was there, wasn't I?" she asked in a whisper.

"Yes, miss, you were. And I, for one, think there's some substance to your story. I've just given you the official evaluation I was told to give you. My boss said the accusations could very well be a devious scheme thought up by one of Chambers' campaign opponents in the gubernatorial race, hoping that an FBI investigation of Chambers' activities might be leaked to the press.

Now that I've given you the department's official recommendation, I'd like to give you my personal one." His voice softened. "As I said, I think there's substance to your story. Although we have nothing concrete to build on, I think I have a few leads. I'll work on the case, quietly, on my own time if you'll agree to help me."

"Let me think this out," Lacy whispered. She stared blankly at the screen for a minute. Finally, she spoke. "Mr. Bryson, Jim Chambers has asked me to marry him. It's probably the most desirable proposal any girl could hope for, but for me it's posed a horrible dilemma.

"Miss Blair, I can't pretend I hadn't heard of your romance with Chambers. That's one reason I need your help. By being his fiancée, you could get closer to Chambers than anybody. Do you think for love of God and country and all that you could tell Chambers you'd marry him and set a far-off wedding date?"

Her stomach flipped. "I don't know...He's so well known, he'd have to announce it, and everybody in the state would know, and then what if,..you know, if I changed my mind..." She kept thinking about Mike Talamino, the only man she'd ever wanted to marry.

"What does it matter what other people think? It's your life."

"I suppose you're right. Jim *would* trust me more if I said I'd marry him."

"Then you'll do it?"

"I don't know." She sat quietly watching the film but not really watching it. When it was over, she turned to him. "I'll do it."

"Still got my card?"

She nodded.

"Good. You can reach me anytime day or night. I want you to contact me between four and seven each evening. But don't call from work, home, or your cell. Make certain no one's watching you. It's a good idea to rotate pay phones. If you were to use the same one each day it would be noticed."

She rose and left. Alone. And she had never felt more alone.

* * *

The following day Lacy was typing a letter when Jim stuck his head into her office.

"I just got in from Dallas. Thought I'd peek in on you."

"Nice to have you back, Jim." She flashed him a bright smile and waved her arm toward a nearby chair, beckoning him to sit there.

"It's good to be back." He sat down. "What are you doing?"

"Oh, just answering questions for a student doing a research paper on the committee system in the Senate. After a few days of this tedium I'll be willing to write a fifteen-thousand-word speech."

"Maybe you won't have to write anything much longer. You know the wife of the lieutenant governor can just concentrate on being beautiful. Beauty shops every day, buying clothes whenever she wants, and lots of traveling. Have you given any more thought to the idea?"

"Yes, Jim." She hesitated, then smiled, and reached out for his hand—all the while her stomach knotted. "I'd like to marry you."

"This is the happiest moment of my life." He pulled her toward him. "Come sit on my lap."

Lacy quietly obliged. She sat sideways and gently settled her head on his shoulders. He wrapped both arms around her and held her tightly against him, then he sought her lips with his own.

Afterward, he spoke. "I can't explain it, but I didn't expect you'd have me. I mean, you've just never seemed any too eager about . . . about us."

"Oh, silly, you're supposed to pursue. My mother told me never to chase a guy. It's a fact that what you don't have always looks better than what you have; hence, your desire for me. I didn't think I stood a chance with you when you could have any woman you want."

"But you're the only one." He kissed her again.

Lacy still hoped his kisses could arouse her, but they didn't. Not like Mike's always had. As she sat there on Jim Chambers' lap, she couldn't keep from thinking of Mike. She'd always known he was THE one for her. So why had she allowed him to get away?

She hoped Jim wasn't aware of her insincerity.

He seemed satisfied.

"Is today okay with you for a wedding?"

"Silly. We hardly know each other."

"How long have you been with me now? Two years?"

"I mean *really* know each other, Jim."

"I suppose you're right."

"What would you say to a three-month courtship?"

"Sounds too long to me." He seized her hand. "But I'd wait three more years if I had to. You know, nothing is going to dissuade me from having you even if you prove to talk with your mouth full of food or snore in your sleep."

She grimaced. "How utterly romantic."

"See why I need a good speechwriter? What do you say to having an immediate press conference announcing the good news?" He beamed like a small boy who had just won a Little League championship.

"I've given some thought to the announcement, Jim, and I feel that perhaps we should keep them guessing a while longer. I'd like to keep on working, and it might be little difficult for me with the staff if they thought I had an inside track—so to speak—with you. And since you've already been married, there's no need for a large wedding."

"I agree with you there. I think a quiet one is in order, and it just may be better to issue a brief announcement a couple of weeks before the ceremony. Maybe that way we can avoid some of the fanfare."

"Hopefully so."

"I suppose the first thing to do is pick a date. We'd better get together with J.B. and check my calendar. We'll need to pick a time when I can get away for two solid weeks with you. That I'm going to insist on."

He kissed her again.

She hated the feel of his lips on hers. His kisses did not affect her anything like Mike's had from Day One. There she was, thinking about Mike Talamino again.

Jim drew away.

They stood, then embraced. "I love you," he

said throatily.

For Lacy, the words were hard to say. At last, she crossed her fingers behind his back and said, "I love you, too, Jim."

Her words sobered him. "I've been waiting for that for so long." He dropped his arms, then took her hand, gazing into her eyes. "How about lunch later?"

"Fine."

* * *

On her way home that day she had to check with the FBI agent. After making certain no one was following her, she found a gas station which had a pay phone in front. She got the card bearing his phone number out of her billfold, and checked her watch. It was five-fifty.

Bryson answered on the second ring.

"Mr. Bryson, this is Lacy Blair."

"Yes, I've been expecting your call. Have you found out anything yet?"

"No."

"Well, I didn't expect anything this soon. Tell me, are you a betrothed lady now?"

"Yes, since this morning. We're not going to announce it for a while, though. Only Richard McNally knows."

A short silence ensued. Lacy wanted to ask if he'd found anything, but she feared he might not be able to disclose his findings to her.

As if he knew what she were thinking, he

said, "I haven't found anything definite yet, but I think we're on the right track. I found the two-and-a-half million in the appropriations for the current biennium. Also, I found records for the purchase of land on Sheridan Highway. Half an acre for $1.8 million."

"That's gotta be that old church! No way it cost even a hundred thousand!"

"There's also a notice on the comptroller's website saying the records were being audited and wouldn't be available for several weeks."

"That sounds awfully suspicious."

"Yep. I've also been looking into Ruth Chambers' death. Something fishy there. The investigating police officer of the accident was killed by sniper fire a couple of weeks after her death. It's nothing concrete, but I'll keep plodding along until I get something. Remember, call me at this number any time, day or night."

"Will do. By the way, I won't be calling you over the weekend. The McNallys and I are going to spend the weekend with Jim at his lake house."

She dreaded being that close to Jim. How could she keep him from wanting to sleep with her?

Chapter 8

Jim's lake house was only a short drive from Austin, but they would not be able to get there until three o'clock Saturday afternoon because of Jim's busy schedule.

The McNallys, Jim and Lacy made the trip in McNally's Mercedes. It was a miserable trip. McNally's car air conditioner went out, and it was a sultry, humid day. They opened the windows. Waves of warm breezes kept them comfortable—and ruined her hair. The sun-baked local terrain seemed to amplify their sensation of roasting. The once-green roadside grass was bleached straw color now by the blistering sun. Pieces of broken glass along the roadside caught the sun's rays and cast back piercing reflections.

Lacy was totally impressed with her first glimpse inside the house. Situated on a hillside fronting the lake, the house had few rooms, but they were each huge, open spaces with soaring ceilings. A glass wall facing the lake gave on to a red-flagstone terrace which ran the length of the house. The terrace, a series of descending platforms, eventually reached the lake and boat dock.

The small party was greeted by a maid Jim introduced as Flo. Jim asked her to prepare the McNallys a drink while he showed Lacy the house.

He guided Lacy through the three-bedroom house, explaining that the first bedroom, one with an accompanying study, was his. The middle room had been his wife's. He merely let Lacy look into the room from the hallway and quickly shut the door, explaining that she could look over the room later, since that was where she would sleep. The third room was the guest room where the McNallys would sleep.

He concluded the tour in the sprawling living room where they were reunited with the McNallys, who sat in a shady spot in the large room, sipping margaritas. Just as Lacy and Jim settled on the L-shaped sofa, Flo appeared with two more margaritas.

This room completely captured Lacy's attention. It ran the length of the lake side of the house. From any point in the room, majestic views of the lake dominated. Next to the view, Lacy liked the way the architect reflected the rustic charm of the hill country in this room. It radiated a ranchy quality in its exposed beam cathedral ceilings and forged-iron light fixtures. The elegance of a baby grand piano, which occupied one end of the long room, clashed with the earthiness the architect had achieved.

Lacy's eyes rested on the piano. "Do you play, Jim?"

"No, Ruth did."

They sat silent for a moment.

Jim broke the chill. "I guess we're all tired and sticky. Why don't we go to our rooms and wash up and rest? I'll get Flo to help you with your things, Lacy," Jim said as he started for the kitchen. "Can you find the room okay?"

Lacy laughed. "I think so, even if I didn't bring my Girl Scout compass." She found the room incompatible with the picture of Ruth Chambers that had been painted by her husband. Lacy had not really known Mrs. Chambers. It was widely repeated that Mrs. Chambers did not care for living in the lieutenant governor's apartment adjacent to the Senate chambers in the Capitol building. She had spent a great deal of her time here at her lake retreat.

The room was utterly feminine and homey. The room's white iron bed featured the sturdy look of an antique hospital bed. No lacy iron work for her. The bedside table of white enamel evoked something from an old doctor's office. All the linens were white.

A built-in bookcase near the window caught Lacy's eye. She walked over to it and examined some of the volumes. Lacy was surprised at Ruth Chambers' taste. Most of the books were collections of poetry, not deep or metaphysical, but mostly ballads and light romantic poems by unknown poets. Many of them were nicely bound first editions, many of them privately published and autographed by the authors. Amidst these books Lacy was pleased to spot a slim volume of East Texas folklore. It was written by E. Donald Blair, Lacy's father.

A quick rap sounded at her door, then Flo entered the room. "Ma'am, I'll draw your bath." She disappeared into the adjoining bathroom.

Lacy rummaged through her suitcase for her terry cloth robe and found it as Flo reentered the room. "Honey, let me unpack for you." She opened the door to the empty closet. "I'll hang your things up in here and iron anything that needs it."

"Oh, I'm sure that won't be necessary. They've been packed scarcely two hours." Lacy wanted to get Flo's impressions of the unfortunate Mrs. Chambers. "Was this Mrs. Chambers' room?" She knew full well it was.

"Yes, ma'am."

"I understand she spent a good deal of time here."

Flo stopped hanging clothes. The blouse she had been hanging she now clutched to her breast. Her gaze seemed fixed on a far-away object. Almost as if she were thinking aloud, she began, "She loved it here. She'd sit out on the terrace for hours, just readin' and writin'. And she'd work in her garden—it's all gone now. I had meant to keep it up for her, but it takes more time and knowhow than I got. She was always takin' in stray pets. I think her biggest disappointment in life was not havin' any youngins." Flo put the blouse on its hanger.

"You were very fond or her, weren't you?"

"Oh, yes, ma'am. She was a kind lady. She loved to cook, and she'd work right along side of me in the kitchen. She taught me more 'bout cookin' than my own mama. Yes," she said thoughtfully, "she was a whole lot different from her husband. They was sure a strange couple. She was always so happy until he would come home. Then she be in kind of a bad mood. And I'll tell you, girl, when he was here I always had two beds to make."

"Are any of Mrs. Chambers' things still here?"

"No, Mr. Chambers boxed 'em all up himself. Her clothes, photographs, and writings—she wrote poetry, you know."

"No, I didn't."

"Well, not many people did. She wrote under one of them pen names."

"I'd love to see some of her work. Is any here?"

"Not that I know of. Mr. Chambers carted it all off. He got rid of all of it."

"What did he do with it?"

"Well, I'll tell you that man's a strange one. He must have taken her death pretty hard, 'cause he took everything she owned way out to the back of the place and burned 'em. If you asks me, it served him right if he grieved her so bad, 'cause he didn't treat her too lovingly when she was alive."

"You said she published a book. What was her pen name?"

"Let me see. What was it? Laura. Laura...I don't remember the last name. Something like Windsong, but I just don't remember."

"Do you remember who published it?"

"All I knows is she paid for it herself. Seems like she had about 300 copies made. She belonged to a poetry club and exchanged books with other members. We was always getting them little books in the mail."

She went to the connecting bathroom. "Your bath be ready, ma'am, and I'd better get back to the kitchen."

Lacy had removed her shoes and jewelry. "Thank you, Flo."

"Oh, I almost forgot to tell you Mr. Chambers said he's going to personally barbecue steaks tonight, and he really knows how to barbecue. He said to come down to the terrace 'bout six o'clock."

Once she was alone in the room, Lacy slipped out of her clothes and got into the bath. She desperately needed to shampoo and blow dry her hair after their windy car ride.

Following the bath, she donned her terrycloth robe, and blew her hair dry, then found her mystery novel, which Flo had thoughtfully placed on the nightstand.

She opened the drapes, filling the room with sunlight. Not another house could be seen.

She curled up on the bed, read the remaining chapters of her book and dozed off. When she awoke, hands on the bedside clock pointed to five-fifty. Lacy leapt from the bed, retrieving her makeup bag on the way to the bathroom. Hurriedly, she applied her makeup, ran a brush through her hair, and dressed.

At six o'clock straight up, she nonchalantly strolled on to the terrace.

"Have a nice rest?" Jim asked her.

"Yes. So nice, in fact, that I nearly didn't make it here—I just woke up."

"If this is the way you look when you wake up, I know I'm going to have a great wife," he said as he handed her a margarita.

Lacy sniffed the air in an exaggerated fashion. "Flo was certainly right about your barbecue, Jim. It smells fantastic. I don't think I'll be able to wait."

"You've still got half an hour of margaritas before you're ready for Big Jim's treat."

"Our poor stomachs are already churning." Lacy selected a seat by the McNallys.

Vivian McNally wore a turquoise cotton sun

top and floral skirt. She had miraculously repaired the damage to her hair. She smelled of a light floral scent and looked as if she had spent the entire day in a beauty shop.

McNally soon left his wife and Lacy to chat with Jim.

"This is the first time we've been here since dear Ruth's death," Vivian said. "We were here the weekend before her death—poor thing." She paused, just as Flo had done when recounting long-stored memories of Ruth Chambers.

"Did you know her well?" Lacy asked.

"I don't think anyone knew her well. She was sort of...well sort of an odd duck. Very quiet. Of course it struck me as unusual that she didn't care anything for the public life. Most women, you must admit, find it glamorous. But Ruth hated it, I do believe."

"Would you know. . ." Lacy hesitated, "if they were happily married?"

"I suppose they were in their own way. After all you couldn't live with a man for ten years and not love him. But it was a strange match. Jim's so gregarious, and she was such an introvert. I think he would have been happier with someone better suited for him—someone like yourself—but, to my knowledge, he never fooled around with other women."

Maybe not physically. But he had lusted for another woman, Lacy thought.

"By the way, Lacy, I haven't had the

opportunity to congratulate you on your engagement. Richard and I both think it's a great match. Also, the family image is so much better for Jim's career than the dashing bachelor one."

Lacy smiled. "I certainly hope there are other reasons than that for the marriage."

"Oh, I didn't mean it to sound like that. As a matter of fact, Richard says Jim is absolutely crazy over you."

Lacy looked into her lap. She could not meet Vivian's eyes. "I'm crazy about him, too."

"How do you like it here?" Vivian asked.

"I love it. I hate to sound anti-social, but it's so wonderfully isolated."

"I don't think it's anti-social to want to get away from civilization for awhile. You've got to unwind from the pressures of this highly mechanized society."

"You and Richard have a weekend place, too, don't you?"

Vivian nodded. "That's why I know what it is to be wonderfully isolated. Our hideaway down on the Gulf is more isolated than this. Our closest neighbor's a mile away, and we have no phone. Rich and I go there and forget there's an outside world.

"When we're there, there's just the two of us on the earth..." she trailed off, as if she were afraid she would reveal too much of her inner self.

Shortly before dinner Flo pushed a serving

cart onto the terrace and unloaded a big salad, Texas toast, dishes, silverware, napkins and condiments onto one of the glass-topped wrought iron tables.

Jim put his arm on Flo's shoulder. "My steaks without Flo's trimmings would be like spaghetti without the meatballs." He looked down at his beaming housekeeper. "Thanks a lot, Flo."

"Just doin' my job, Mr. Chambers."

"I'd like to take her back to Austin with me," Lacy said.

Flo had a smile on her face as she returned to the house.

"She'll be yours to command soon enough," Jim said. "Just think. Mrs. Lacy Chambers. How does that sound?"

"Very nice," Lacy said, placing the inflection on very.

Throughout dinner, they suffered through flies buzzing around them, but when the mosquitoes came out, they moved into the living room.

Jim mixed another round or drinks, then asked if anyone could play the piano.

Both McNallys shook their heads. After a long pause, Lacy said, "I play a little. Despite four years of piano lessons, I still play poorly."

"Let's have a sing along," Jim said.

Lacy took a seat on the piano bench and was surprised there was no sheet music. Had he burned it, too? Jim came to sit beside her as Richard claimed his wife's hand.

With the four of them gathered around the piano, Jim quickly made a request. "Since you all are UT grads, can you start with *The Eyes of Texas*?"

She obliged, and they all sang.

His next request was *Dixie*.

She followed by playing *You Can't Always Get What You Want*.

By the time they gone through a half a dozen songs, they were giggling like junior high girls at a slumber party. Hands still clasped, the McNallys were exchanging lovesick glances with one another.

The foursome returned to the sofa to watch the last of the day's sunset over the shimmering lake. They spoke of the governor's race and sipped drinks until midnight when Jim suggested the ladies retire. "You girls must be dead tired. Rich and I have some things to talk over, but y'all better saw some logs. C'mon, Lacy, I'll walk you to your room."

The hallway lights were dim. When they reached Lacy's door Jim took her in his arms. He stood there holding her tightly for what seemed to Lacy like ten minutes. At last, he kissed her. It was long and very tender. And she wished she were kissing Mike. Why had she let herself get into this situation with Jim? She was filled with self loathing.

He whispered, "Oh, Lacy . . . I want you so. May I come to your room later?"

Still clutching him, Lacy remained silent. She felt as if he could surely hear her racing heart. She felt as if she had to swallow, but she couldn't. Finally, she answered him with a firm shake of her head.

After a short pause, he said, "Oh, angel, if you won't give in to me on this, you'll have to give in to me on the wedding date. Let's move it up."

Surprised, Lacy asked, "How much closer?"

"The soonest we could manage is six weeks away. How about it?"

"If that's what you want, Jim."

"I'd also like to hear you tell me you love me."

She swallowed. Her heartbeat roared. "Okay, silly, I love you."

He hugged her tightly. "I love you, you silly angel. Now I think you had better get some sleep. Breakfast will be served at nine on the terrace. Wear your swimming things because we'll go out in the boat before returning to Austin." He touched her nose with his fingertips. "Good night, angel."

Lacy slipped into her nightgown, planning to take Jim's advice and get some sleep, but she felt very much awake. Again, she was drawn to the bookcase of the hauntingly mysterious Ruth Chambers. Lacy hoped she could find there some clue as to the peculiar marriage, perhaps some insight into Ruth Chambers' view of her husband. Lacy examined each book. None were written by a Laura. None contained any loose slips of unfinished poetry. Lacy searched the dresser drawers. Nothing. She fruitlessly looked beneath the mattress. The closet had been empty, but Lacy nevertheless felt along the top shelf. Nothing again. She looked in vain in the bathroom.

Scarcely a sign that she ever occupied the room, thought Lacy. She was puzzled over her own obsession to find out what Ruth Chambers really had been like.

She settled in the bed and tried to sleep, but was wide awake, thinking of Jim. It was funny, she thought, how she could have idolized for over two years this man who now, day by day, was crumbling before her eyes. Each day she was finding glaring flaws in his character which had escaped her notice during the two years she had been blinded by overwhelming admiration for him.

She had never before noticed, for instance, what a megalomaniac he was. She knew all politicians possessed enlarged egos; that much she could dismiss. But tonight he had completely dominated the conversation. McNally had uttered scarcely a dozen words. And at the conclusion of each song that evening, Jim had belted out another of his never-ending requests, never asking if anyone else cared to exercise a choice. Lacy realized now that out of the office, he still continued to treat McNally and her as his employees.

Now, for the first time, she thought she could dislike him. He cared for nothing but his own dictatorial notions. If—and there was little in the way of a challenge—he should be elected governor in November, he would use the governorship only as a stepping stone to bigger things. He was merely biding time in Texas, waiting until his thirty-fifth birthday when he would be old enough for the presidency or vice presidency. He had the money, machine, and charisma for the office. But how dangerous it was for a man like him to hold any kind of public office.

Never before in her life had she been so lonely and miserable. Everything she had always dreamed of was now turned upside down, out of proportion like in a bad dream. Here she was, twenty-five, engaged to a man she had to force herself to say she loved, to a man she suspected of the most loathsome deeds. No matter what she and the FBI investigator would prove, she could never marry Jim Chambers. She only hoped she would not have to keep up her charade much longer.

Her mind was too crammed with details of the blurred mess of a predicament she was in. It was no use hoping for sleep. It could not come until she freed her mind. Remembering some magazines on the coffee table in the living room, Lacy decided to get them to ease her into sleep. She looked at her watch. Two o'clock.

She tiptoed in her foam-soled slippers down the dark hall to the end, not wanting to disturb the sleepers. When she reached the end of the hall she heard soft men's voices from the bar in the living room.

She pivoted to return to her room when she heard a few words from the indistinguishable voices. She heard "comptroller" and "FBI." She abruptly stopped, trying not to breathe, straining to hear better. Then she heard, "snooping...day care funds...old church wasn't worth a hundred grand." At this point, she heard the two walking back toward the couch, their words becoming impossible to understand.

Now, she knew. All hope was gone. Her former hero was hopelessly tarnished.

Her shock and disappointment turned to sudden wrath. *Too bad I don't have a tape recorder,* she thought. She listened more attentively but still could not make out anything.

Terror struck her when she heard her own name mentioned. How much could they know? They could surmise that Bryson had not come snooping until after her trip to Schneiderburg. She felt sick inside at her perilous position, but still she stood there in the darkness of the hall, eagerly waiting to hear pieces of their conversation.

She could not have estimated how long she stood there. It seemed like hours. Not being able to grasp the conversation, she could not tell when it was being terminated. One minute she heard them softly speaking, the next they were crossing the room. She had never really known fear until this minute.

Chapter 9

Her heart thudding violently, Lacy scurried toward her room, fervently praying that she escape detection. Just as she heard Jim's and McNally's footsteps on the hallway tiles, she slipped into her bedroom, not quite closing the door for fear of noise. She raced across the carpet and flung herself on the bed, pulling the covers over her—robe and slippers and all.

A few hours later, in spite of a dull headache from loss of sleep, Lacy climbed out of bed. It was seven o'clock. After throwing on a cotton skimmer and sandals, she sneaked from her room and down the hall, pausing at Jim's door. She heard a hardy snore and went on through the kitchen and out the back door.

Flo had said Jim crated up all his wife's things and carried them to the rear of the property where he burned them. The rear three or four acres were rocky bush that had never been landscaped. Lacy zigzagged through the bush, carefully scanning the dew-covered ground for evidence of a small bonfire. A frog's sudden croak frightened her into a leap.

When she met a low rock wall, she knew she had reached the end of Jim's land. She slowly stepped over each square foot of earth between the rock wall and the road which had brought them there the day before.

Halfway to the highway she came upon a mound of growth. Intermingled in the heap were metal picture frames from which the pictures had been removed, cosmetic jars and perfume bottles, buttons and buckles.

Lacy looked toward the house. Luckily a large tree stood between her and the house, blocking her from view of the house. She stooped down to examine the pile more closely.

The wild grass covering the mound of rubble was not deeply rooted. Soot and charred objects settled under the mound's small summit. Lacy's fingers carefully combed through the ashes and dirt, pushing aside the larger items which had originally caught her eye. She dug deeper, using her fingers as a sifter. She felt another small metal object. After closer examination, it proved to be a small lock, the variety used on teenaged girls' diaries. She was close to the bottom and had found nothing of interest. Then, she felt a tiny metal box. It was heavy in her hand. She pulled it out and saw that it was a pearl-studded pill box. Her heart sank at the thought of finding a note inside. After several seconds of fidgeting with the rusty catch, she managed to open it. It was empty.

She was certain she had combed through the whole hump. Next, she carefully examined its periphery. Nothing. She got to her feet.

Her trip had been wasted.

Back in the house, she paused again at Jim's door. He was still snoring. She checked her watch. Her jaunt had taken only twenty-five minutes.

She didn't waste any time when she reached her room. First, she washed her filthy hands. She gave her fingernails a once-over with clear polish. She had to use a white pencil under her nails to restore them. Then she plugged in her curling iron, and while it was heating, she shaved her legs. After fixing her hair, she applied the minimal makeup that she wore.

During those sleepless hours before dawn she had done a lot of thinking. She decided she needed to try to convince Jim of her love so she could get evidence which could convict him in court. Jim Chambers had to be stopped. Would she have to be the one to bring him down? How had she ever gotten herself into such a nightmare?

When she was completely satisfied with her appearance, she slipped into a flattering, yet not too revealing, red bikini. With it, she wore a white eyelet coverlet and white sandals.

She beat the McNallys to breakfast and caught Jim sitting alone. She put her arm around him, leaned over, and gave him a warm kiss. "Good morning, sweetheart."

His eyes ran over her approvingly, then he pulled her down on his lap. "You've just made me one heck of a happy guy."

"Hey, you two lovebirds, save that for the honeymoon." It was Richard McNally, with Vivian at his side.

Lacy started to get up, but Jim pulled her back.

"Don't let him scare you away. I, personally, was just getting comfortable."

She remained on his lap until Flo rolled out the breakfast cart and began to place its contents on the table. There was a carafe of hot coffee, a basket of steaming biscuits, a platter of sausage patties, a bowl of scrambled eggs, and four grapefruit halves in serving dishes.

"Flo, you've really outdone yourself. Everything smells delicious," Jim said as Flo placed the contents of the cart on the table. "Just put them there, and we can help ourselves."

"Did you make the biscuits from scratch?" Lacy asked.

"Yes, ma'am," Flo said. "Nothin' better than homemade buttermilk biscuits."

From her chair on the terrace, Lacy eyed

the shimmering, crystal-like lake.

After breakfast she got to see the lake up close when the foursome went out on the boat. The water was clear enough to disclose schools of fish meandering by. Jim told her the water was extremely deep and not recommended for the casual swimmer. Great masses of inaccessible granite bordered the east side of the lake. The north shore was so distant it still could not be seen.

"Hey, I really like this new boat, Jim," McNally said.

Vivian cast a mischievous glance at Lacy. "By the way, Lacy, I hope you can swim. Last year when we were here our skillful captain nearly drowned his poor wife—busted the boat up to smithereens. Poor Ruth couldn't even swim. Luckily, she snatched a piece of the wreckage to keep her afloat until Jim got to her."

McNally and Jim exchanged serious glances. "Now, Viv, in all fairness, you must admit Jim's a strong swimmer and Ruth was in no real danger," McNally said.

"Oh, I know, dear, but I thought I'd tease Jim and warn Lacy to prepare for disaster when Jim's at the helm." She glanced at Jim. "I do hope your new boat came with operating instructions."

"Yes, Vivian." Jim was visibly annoyed.

Vivian McNally's remarks had cast a cloud over the excursion. McNally and Jim remained silent, Jim never leaving the helm.

Lacy could think of nothing but last year's accident. Had Jim tried to kill his wife? Lacy could not ignore the possibility. Funny how she could be so detached now toward the man she had worshipped only a week before.

It was a shame Jim destroyed his wife's things. Knowing Ruth Chambers' attraction to writing poetry, Lacy knew she must have recorded her fears in verse. But no one would ever know now.

The Central Texas skies seemed to take their cue from the gloomy foursome. Charcoal clouds blanketed the sky as gusty winds slapped the now-choppy lake.

"It's a good thing we're close to the dock. If we were out in the middle now we'd be in a pretty dangerous fix," Jim said. "I should be able to dock before rain falls."

Lacy's eyelet cover-up offered no protection against the chilly winds. She hugged herself to keep warm. Jim glanced at her and started to shed his windbreaker. "Here, take this."

"I most certainly will not. You need it." She paused. "Hey, why don't I get in there with you?"

His eyes danced with delight.

Lacy edged her back into his chest as he pulled one side of the windbreaker around both of them. His right arm encircled the top of her body.

Lacy smiled as she looked up at him. "The

body heat really helps."

In spite of the cumbersomeness of Lacy's bulk wedged against him, Jim maneuvered the boat with the skill of a superior boatman. Lacy knew last summer's boating incident was no accident.

Chapter 10

Monday proved to be the longest work day Lacy could ever remember. She could not wait to tell Bryson the skimpy details of the overheard conversation between Jim and McNally. The agent might also be interested in last summer's boating mishap.

As she drove around the Capitol after work, she noticed a blue car with two men in it behind her. The car still followed a half mile later. Perhaps she was being overly cautious, she told herself. But Bryson had cautioned her to be certain no one followed before she called him.

So, certain she would be.

Since she was close to a small, out-of-the-way book shop she frequented, she decided to stop there. Then she could determine if she were being followed. She turned left. The blue car, which lagged three of four cars behind her, slowly rounded the corner after her. Two blocks down, she turned right. Driving very slowly, she kept checking the rear-view mirror. The blue car also turned right. She inched her car up to a parallel parking spot in front of the book shop. She was trembling now.

As she turned off the engine, she searched her mirror, trying to identify the men. The driver wore a white shirt, dark suit and tie. His hair was grey. The other man would be easy to spot again. He was redheaded, young and wore shirt sleeves with no tie.

As she entered the shop, she saw the blue car drive by slowly. She felt as if she were in a fishbowl. She was the only customer in the shop. She darted for the bookcases which displayed works of English fiction when the poetry section caught her eye. She stopped in front of it. Her eyes quickly scanned the familiar titles, then stopped on one slim volume. Its title was *Tarnished*. The poetess was Laura Windsong. Her heart pounding with excitement, Lacy snatched it away. She looked at the flyleaf, hoping to find an inscription. There was none.

Her concentration on the book broke when the door opened. She looked over the shelves. It was the redhead. Icy fear penetrated into every pore of her body. She followed him with her eyes without moving her head. He was careful not to look her in the face. Going directly to the rear of the shop, he selected a spot from which he could watch her every movement.

She seized this moment to pay for the book.

Lacy thought the cashier concentrated a bit too much on her trembling hands. "By the way," Lacy said, trying to divert her attention, "I've been trying to locate the 1906 collection of Governor Hogg's speeches. Seems you can't get one outside of the archives. Is there any possibility of you locating one?" She knew the few volumes in existence belonged to private collectors.

"You can leave your name and number, and I'll let you know if I hear of one coming available," the clerk said.

Lacy jotted down the information and left.

Still shaking as she took the driver's seat, she quickly locked her door. She had difficulty finding the keys. Before starting the car she searched the block for the blue car. It was not visible. As she started the car, she saw the redhead peering at her from the book store window.

She left the street far more quickly than she had entered. Rounding the corner, she spotted the blue car. The driver's face was hidden behind a map.

Before she reached the main intersection two blocks up, she saw through her rear-view mirror the young redhead get in the blue car. Throughout the next two miles, the blue car followed her, keeping several car lengths behind. Lacy knew she would not be able to call Bryson. A call from a pay phone would look too suspicious.

Why were they following her? Could it have something to do with Jim suspecting her of alerting Bryson? She felt sure Jim was responsible for the two men tagging her. Could she be sure the men were simply following her and recording her activities? Then a bizarre—but terrifying—thought seized her. Could they be murderers contracted to kill her? She suddenly imagined the redhead pulling the trigger of a high-powered rifle, aiming it at her head at that very minute. Should she risk going home where she could be cornered by the two watchdogs? She thought of Jim. He was still very much attracted to her, in love with her in his own peculiar way. He would not have her killed unless he had caught her at something. They couldn't have caught her at anything yet, though no one but she could have contacted the FBI. She reassured herself that she was just being followed.

Knowing her dangerous predicament, she felt the safest course would be to act naturally, to go directly home.

Safe in her house—alone—she could let her terror subside. After securing the deadbolt lock on both front and back doors, she tried to exercise calm reasoning. It was a case of mind over matter. She was safe in the confines of her house. She now knew her enemy, which put her a step ahead of them. She would not do anything foolish.

When night fell, she looked out of her bedroom window without being seen. As she suspected, the blue car parked several houses down the street from hers. She supposed they would stay there all night, or at least until a replacement arrived.

Now that she was certain she was being watched, she could not rule out wiretapping. Anyone capable of illegal wiretapping could also have planted bugs in her house. For no reason would she consider calling Bryson from home, nor could she risk calling him from her office.

She then remembered the ladies' room at a local department store had a pay phone in it. She planned to go there the following day on her lunch hour. At least her watchdogs would not be able to follow her in there.

She ate a bacon sandwich and settled down to read Ruth Chambers' poetry book. It took her only an hour and a half to read it. On the whole, Ruth Chambers' work represented to Lacy a pitifully amateurish effort. Both in subject matter and in banal phraseology, all of the poems were trite. Lacy could tell that Ruth Chambers had been a deeply religious woman. Many of the poems were inspirational. For the insight into Ruth Chambers' life, the poems were valuable. The poem Lacy reread the most dealt with a shattered marriage—shattered because the husband was not what the wife thought he was.

In the poem Lacy found the most enlightening, Ruth Chambers had apparently found her husband guilty of:

Sins which would surely guarantee
This man I had loved
A horrendous eternity.

She had concluded the poem with:

Though I live in deepest strife,
I'll keep His binds
Until He concludes this life.

This was the closest Lacy had come to finding tangible evidence to use against Jim Chambers. The book publisher was bound to have a record of who paid for the private printing. Lacy could also seek out the poetry society that Ruth Chambers had belonged to and find members who might be able to identify her, if not by name, at least by the lake address or by her photo.

Lacy realized the pseudonym and the fact the accusations (sins) against Jim were vague would pose a legal problem, but it would be something to start with. She could scarcely wait until she could give her newly found leads to Bryson the next day.

After she turned out her bedside lamp, she

went to her window and peeked out. The blue car had swapped with a white one. A lone man sat in the white car, taking advantage of full view of Lacy's house.

Chapter 11

The headline on the bottom of page one of her newspaper arrested Lacy's attention the following morning. *FBI agent found dead.* Her heart pounding furiously, she read on, hoping against hope it was not Bryson.

An agent for the Federal Bureau of Investigation was shot dead early Tuesday in his parked car at 503 First St.

Police seek two men who were seen fleeing from the scene in a late model dark blue car.

Joseph Bryson, an FBI agent assigned to Austin, was pronounced dead on arrival at Breckinridge Hospital at 12:30 a.m. He suffered a bullet wound to the head.

Police were summoned to the area by two students who heard gunshots while walking to their cars after seeing a band on Sixth Street.

Also late Monday, Bryson's office in the Federal Building was ransacked, leaving police no clues as to the nature of the case Bryson was working on at the time of his death. A local FBI spokesman said Bryson was "between cases."

Numb all over, Lacy laid down the paper. She regretted their decision to shoulder the dangerous suspicions alone. What else could she have done? Intuition had told her from the start that investigating the Hispanic girl's accusations could be a deadly business.

Not only was Bryson dead, but his office had been broken into. Had he written anything about her? What was that peculiar shorthand he had recorded the day of their first meeting? Had they gotten that last night? If only she knew what Bryson's files had held on her. She could very well be marked for the same fate which had taken Bryson's life.

Suddenly she remembered she had Bryson's phone number in her billfold. She had meant to memorize and destroy it from the very first, but it was one of the things she never got around to doing.

She got the billfold from her purse, took out the crisp card and flushed it down the toilet. Watching it disappear into the sewage, Lacy felt her last hope was perishing with that tiny slip of paper.

Like a thunderclap had awakened her, she realized her own life was drastically threatened. It was as if Jim had cut off her oxygen supply to force her to surface. She would be followed every minute. Her every phone call would be monitored. And if she attempted to get help, to jeopardize Jim Chambers' vast political empire, her life would be snuffed out.

What was she to do? She knew her phone wires had to be tapped. If she placed a call now, she'd probably be dead before help arrived. If she drove for help, the minute she stepped out of the car, say at a police station, she would be gunned down just as Bryson had been.

Perhaps she could somehow manage to smuggle out a letter. This last idea gave her encouragement.

She went to her computer, and as quickly as she could type, she wrote her entire story, starting with the trip to Schneiderburg. She included details of her meeting with Bryson, her overheard conversation between McNally and Jim, Ruth Chambers' poetry, and concluded with the account of being followed by the two men in the blue car, the men who matched the description of Bryson's killers. Although she used abbreviations, incomplete sentences and people's initials after the first reference, the letter still ran twelve pages.

But who would be trustworthy enough to receive the letter? State employees were out of the question. Jim had some sort of hold over most of them.

She considered sending it to the FBI in Washington, but was afraid it would never reach the right people while she was still alive. If only she knew someone who owed no allegiance to Jim Chambers. That left out most of her friends. And though Becky's loyalty would be only to Lacy, since she was Lacy's roommate, they probably watched her closely already.

Lacy could think of no one. She printed the letter, signed it, and put it in a stamped, blank envelope. Then she basted it to the inside lining of her suit jacket before getting dressed for work.

She had lost all track of time. She would not have been surprised if it were already ten o'clock. She was relieved to find it was only eight. The time she had spent on the letter had been only slightly longer than the time she set aside each morning for reading the newspaper.

Just as she was about to leave, Becky meandered into the room, yawning. She wore an un-ironed shift and sandals. Her hair was a mess.

"Lace, I hate to ask it of you, but my car's on the blink. I'm going to have to put it in the garage at Sears this morning, and I wondered if you could follow me over, then drop me by the university."

"Sure, it's not much out of the way, and the university's not far from Sears. What's the matter with your car?"

"Something in the cooling system. Every time I stop, I have to put water in the dumb thing. Yesterday it made the most awful noise—sounded like the mating call of a dying rhinoceros."

Lacy let out a roaring laugh. "You ought to turn your wit to speechwriting."

"No, thanks. I'm perfectly apolitical. It'd kill me, too, to be part of the establishment."

Becky's car! It might just be the escape vehicle Lacy needed. She was not at all sure how she would manage it, but she had to try. She could work out the details later.

"Do you want me to pick you up about five today, so we can get the car?" Lacy asked.

"You're an angel. That'd be great. If you really don't mind, why don't you pick me up on the Drag in front of the Union?"

"Fine." At least she could plan on the car being there until five. Now, if she could only lose her followers long enough to pick up Becky's car, she could maneuver an escape.

It did not surprise Lacy to see the two watchdogs in the blue car following her again. She kept close watch on them via her rear-view mirror. They obviously were puzzled by her tailgating of Becky. And when she saw the redhead who rode shotgun talking into a cell phone she knew he must be requesting aid to follow Becky.

When they arrived at the Sears auto center, she caught sight of a white car with two men in it tailgating the blue car.

Becky was with the mechanic only a

minute.

Despite the fear which strummed through her, Lacy kept up a typical conversation with Becky all the way to the university. She had to act perfectly natural. Becky must suspect nothing. For Becky's safety, she had to remain ignorant of Lacy's peril.

It was difficult, though, for Lacy to laugh with Becky about yesterday's *Daily Texan* editorial when visions of Bryson's blood-stained body kept blurring her concentration. And it wasn't easy discussing the evening's dinner when she didn't know if she'd be alive at dinner time.

When she arrived at the Capitol, she could not imagine what was going on. Newsmen's cars and TV mobile units were all over the grounds. Her first thought was that FBI agents had exposed Jim. She could hardly wait to find out what the big news was.

As soon as she entered the building, photographic flashes blinded her. She then realized the newsmen were taking *her* picture. She did not know why, and she did not want to ask. She kept walking. The newsmen continued to follow her, tossing questions all along.

She soon grasped the gist of their interest in her. She heard repeated, *Congratulations, Lacy. Any comment on the Lieutenant Governor's announcement?*

How long are you going to remain working for Mr. Chambers?

She did not smile. *Oh, God, it must be the wedding announcement.* She briskly walked straight to Jim's office.

His secretary said, "Congratulations, Lacy."

"Thanks. Jim in?"

"Yes. Go right on in."

Lacy almost slammed the door behind her. He was alone. "What's the idea of announcing this without my knowledge?"

"I told you Saturday night I was going to move up the wedding date. I saw nothing wrong in announcing it to the press."

"Did it ever occur to you that I'd rather tell my mother about it before she heard it on the radio?"

"I'm sorry, Lacy. I hadn't thought of that."

"I also think we should have made the announcement together. Why couldn't you have waited another thirty minutes?"

"Guess I just wanted to surprise you."

"Surprise! I couldn't imagine what was going on. When I walked in the building I was mobbed. I didn't even know why. I was terribly rude, not to mention being noncommittal. I didn't know, for example, when my own wedding date is. Don't you think I'm entitled to have a hand in the preparations?" She was shouting.

"Honestly, Lacy, I'm sorry. It's just that you led me to believe you didn't care about the details of the wedding. I only meant to surprise you. Now, why don't you take the day off and go shopping for a trousseau? You've only got three weeks to get ready."

"Three weeks! Oh, Jim, that's not nearly long enough. I've got to figure out guest lists, get invitations to the printers, plan everything, shop for a gown and trousseau. It's absolutely impossible." She couldn't subdue her anger.

"You *can* make it. First of all, you don't have to work here anymore. Second, my staff will take care or the invitations. You give them a list of your friends and relatives you'll want at the wedding. If you don't have addresses, don't worry. They'll look them up for you. They'll also plan the reception, flowers and everything. You don't have to worry your pretty little head about anything except being beautiful."

She had to control her anger. The stakes of this game could very well be her life. She must appease him. She smiled and in a soft voice said, "Well, first off, I'll need to evacuate my office. What do you want done with my research files? I've worked so hard to build them up, I almost hate to turn them over to someone else, but I suppose my replacement will need them."

"I guarantee you'll never again need to use those things."

He got up from his desk and came over to

her, kissing her on the cheek. "Make a day of it." He reached into his pocket and pulled out a one-hundred dollar bill. "Here, treat yourself to lunch."

"Oh, Jim, I can't take that."

"Yes, you most certainly can. If you were marrying anyone else, you wouldn't have to go through all of this, so take it. Also, I want you to go shopping." He pulled from his wallet a black American Express card. "You're marrying a rich man. Go buy a trousseau."

She took it. "I'll try not to buy up the whole town. But, first, I think I'll call my mom, clean out my desk, and get a guest list together." She turned to go, then pivoted toward him again. "When will I see you again?"

"This is one hell of a romance. I'm to be at the airport by noon. I'm going to El Paso. Won't be back until late tomorrow night. I'll call you tonight, though."

"Have a nice trip, sweetheart." She blew him a kiss as she left.

The next two hours Lacy gave to sorting out the two years of memorabilia her office stored. Not that it took the full two hours. Her thoughts kept getting enmeshed in the web of circumstances which smothered her. Why, she wondered, had Jim made the announcement this morning? She knew there was a calculated plan behind it. But what kind of plan she was unable to imagine. Also, something about him had been different. He had called her Lacy, something he had not done in private recently. And he kissed her on the cheek, not the lips.

He was planning something for her, and she had no way of seeking help. Her only hope was her letter. And it was indeed a faint hope. To whom could she send it? And how?

While cleaning out her desk, she came across a souvenir postcard she had saved for a couple of years. The photo was of a sign which greets people entering the town of Hondo, Texas. It read: THIS IS GOD'S COUNTRY, DON'T DRIVE THROUGH IT LIKE HELL. Mike Talamino had sent Lacy the post card.

Her thoughts turned to Mike. She wished now she had listened to him two years ago. He had guessed even then that something was not right with Jim Chambers. *Mike's one man Jim could never buy.*

And then she knew Mike Talamino was her only hope.

She looked up Mike's Houston address, hoping there would not be any other attorneys named Michael Talamino listed. There weren't. She ripped the envelope from its secure hiding place in her suit jacket and started to copy his name and address on to it. But she stopped her pen before it touched the envelope. What if she were caught with the letter? She could not jeopardize this innocent man. Perhaps she could think of a code name he'd recognize, but no one else would.

Then she remembered her first date with him. She was living in a girl's dorm which required her to sign out before she left for a date. She was to write down her date's name. She hadn't, at that time, been able to remember the Italian surname of the law student she was going out with, so she had signed him as "Mike Q. Public." Mike and she had quite a laugh over it, and she continued to sign out that way whenever she went out with him.

She addressed the letter to Mike Q. Public at his Houston apartment and put it in her purse.

She had to uncrate reams of paper in the secretarial pool to secure a box to accommodate her office trappings. She hated facing the girls in the secretarial pool. A few were cool toward her; others beamed as they congratulated her and asked personal questions to which Lacy merely tossed her head back and sighed a slight laugh. She wasn't about to act besotted over Jim Chambers for the benefit of these girls.

Back in her office, she gathered up the things she was going to keep from her desk: a pen set given her by Jim, a collegiate dictionary, a Spanish-English dictionary, Bartlett's Familiar Quotations, Roget's Thesaurus, a secretary's handbook, her university degree, a photo of the Capitol, and state stationery which bore her name.

Before closing the door to her office for the last time, she took Mike's letter and tucked it in the side pocket of her purse.

On the way to her car she stopped by the postal station in the Capitol Building. She set down her box and got the letter from her purse. Just as she was about to put it in the out-of-town slot, someone snatched it from her. She looked up quickly.

The redheaded man who stood before her had a sadistic smile on his face.

"From now on, we'll take care of your mail for you, Miss Blair. The Lieutenant Governor wouldn't want you to have to do secretary's work, would he?"

"And who's going to read my mail?" she demanded angrily.

"Whoever said we was going to read it? You must have misunderstood me."

"I think I understand you perfectly."

"In that case, why don't we go see what Mr. Chambers thinks of your letter?"

Knowing how well trapped she was, Lacy did not attempt to get away.

The sudden lift she had gotten from thinking Mike would rescue her had overbuilt her confidence. In her excitement over getting the letter off to Mike, she had completely forgotten to watch for her followers.

It had been the most foolish and costly move she would ever make.

She was escorted to Jim's office by her redheaded captor. He closed Jim's door behind them and stood at the door throughout the grim scene that followed.

Jim read over the letter. She stood there thinking the letter had been her death warrant. There was no escape. What manner of murder would they choose? It could not be as violent as Bryson's. Too many questions. It would have to be something that looked like an accident, she decided. Like Ruth Chambers'.

At last, he looked up from the letter. He was not scowling at her as she had thought he would. Instead, he had a menacing smirk on his face. "I'm not really surprised, you know."

"I know."

"I'm not even going to plead innocent. You're too smart for that. I'll tell you what I'm going to do. I had to have Bryson killed. That was the only way to silence him. But I'd rather not risk any more deaths. There's another way to silence you. I'm going to silence you by marrying you."

Lacy gaped at him in disbelief.

"I said I was going to possess you. It doesn't matter to me if you don't love me. I'll get what I want even if I have to at gunpoint. And you better get used to looking at Pete's red head because it's going to follow you around for the rest of your days."

"That might not be long," she said sarcastically.

"You won't get off that easily, my dear."

"Thanks."

"And, dearest, don't get any ideas about getting in touch with the authorities. Most of them I can buy off. I might add that we are now laying the foundations to use in framing you for a crime. If you ever leave me, I'll have you on death row for it. Now you and Pete run along. You do have a lot of shopping to do, my love. By the way, everyone thinks it's so romantic of me to hire a bodyguard for my bride-to-be. Don't you?"

Not for a minute did she believe she'd live long enough to marry him. This was another of his evil schemes to make himself look like the poor, grieving fiancé when an "accident" claimed her life.

Chapter 12

If Pete was going to be her constant companion, Lacy decided he might as well work. With no regard for price, she charged hundreds of dollars worth of clothes on Jim's cards, and after each purchase, she gave Pete the bags to carry.

"I don't suppose this is your cup of tea," Lacy said to him as she charged a couple of blouses in a chic clothing shop.

Pete completely ignored her remark and stared at her with cold blue eyes. She had no trouble believing he was a murderer.

"Just one more stop now. I've got to pick up some wash cloths and towels at Sears. Then you can see me home."

She needed no wash cloths or towels, but she did need an excuse to get to Sears. At Sears, she purchased a half a dozen white wash cloths and a pair of matching towels. As they got close to the rest rooms, she said, "I've got to go in there now—so sorry you won't be able to follow." She turned on her finest smile as she gave him her bag.

Now for her carefully planned escape.

In the ladies' room, she had to act quickly. She went straight to the window. As far as she knew, this was the only department store in Austin that had a restroom with a window. It was a small one, but with a nearby chair to step on she would be able to manage it.

Unfortunately, she was not alone. A young woman with two small children shared the facilities. Lacy knew she would have to wait until she was alone to make her daring escape. She stood before a mirror brushing her hair, pretending to be intent.

The young mother was having quite a time managing her two toddlers and several packages. Just as Lacy thought they were going to leave, the oldest of the two children, a boy, broke away from his mother. He climbed under a locked door to an out-of-order stall.

"Todd! Come out right this minute," the mother demanded.

"I can't, Mommy. The door won't open."

"Well, get out the way you got in."

"I don't want to. The floor's all dirty."

"If you don't come out right now, I'm going to give you the biggest spanking you ever got."

"Why don't you find the man with the keys? He can let me out."

Lacy's stomach churned. This small guy not more than three years old could stand between her and freedom.

"Okay, Todd, Tammy and I are going to go

find the man with the keys right now. Don't worry if we don't get back for while. I don't think anything will happen to you. Bye-bye." She started for the door.

Just then his little blond head peeked out from below the door, and he came on through. "I decided I could get a little dirty."

The mother winked at Lacy, who was putting the brush back in her purse.

As the outer door was swinging shut, Lacy snatched the chair, put it under the window, and climbed out as if a swarm of bumble bees were chasing her.

No one saw her. She raced to the car service center and told the first attendant she saw that she wanted to pick up her green Kia and that she was in a terrible hurry. He wrote up the bill. It totaled close to ninety dollars. She gave him the one hundred dollar bill Jim had given her, got her change, and drove off in Becky's car.

She immediately got on the expressway. By instinct now, she continuously checked her rear-view mirror. No cars appeared to be following. She had to leave Austin.

San Antonio was the closest city that was large enough to get lost in. It was a little over an hour away.

She couldn't think beyond her immediate danger. What she would do tomorrow was of no concern. She had to remove herself from the heat of the fire. Perhaps its deadly fumes would reach her still, but she could not worry about that now.

During that hour's drive, Lacy never stopped looking into her rear-view mirror. She conjured up visions of highway patrolmen hunting her down. She drove at seventy miles an hour in a seventy zone, so she was in no danger of attracting attention for speeding.

By now Pete would know what car she was in and would probably be giving the license number to area law enforcement agencies. She wondered what sort of story he and Jim would tell about her.

While gazing monotonously into the rear-view mirror, Lacy noticed a pick-up truck with two men wearing cowboy hats. The truck had pulled up behind her at a high rate of speed, but on reaching to within twenty yards or her, it had slowed down, keeping a steady seventy miles-per-hour pace behind her. She considered turning off onto one of the dirt roads dissecting the highway, but decided she would be easy prey on a remote road. It might even be days before her body was found. Her best hope was in quickly reaching the metropolitan area of San Antonio. She accelerated. The speedometer gauged seventy-five, then eighty.

The pick-up slackened off. After a few minutes Lacy saw the truck turn off onto a dirt road.

A false alarm.

If only she had a good friend in San Antonio. Her only acquaintance here, Senator Marshall, was much closer to Jim than he was to her. And besides, he was not home. He was chairing an interim committee in the capital, and his family was staying with him at his Austin hotel. "That's it!" she said to herself.

The senator's address was engraved in her memory from all the times she had sent reports and letters to his house. Thirty-six-twenty-four Waverly Trail.

Fortunately, Becky's car had a GPS system. Once she was approaching the metropolitan area of San Antonio, she got off the freeway and programmed the senator's address into the system.

She had no trouble finding the house. It was in a fairly upscale neighborhood of oversized parcels of land. She was more than grateful that the house sat back from the street on a wooded lot. At least she would not have to worry about prying neighbors who knew the senator's family was out of town.

The car stopped in the drive. She approached the attached three-car garage and tried the doors. They all were locked. She peered in the horizontal silts of glass on the garage doors. The garage sheltered only one car, the senator's sports car. At the back of the garage she saw a door. She went to the rear of the garage. The door was locked but had an odd type of window, more a wood frame enclosing glass panels. The frame was fastened to the door by four screws. The manicure scissors in her purse served well in removing the screws. She easily lifted away the glass. Next, Lacy pushed up a patio chair to use as a ladder and hoisted herself in.

She pressed the garage door opener, then drove her car into the garage and shut and locked the door.

From the garage, she entered the kitchen and found a telephone. After getting the number of a cab company, she called and asked for a cab to pick her up at the corner of Waverly Trail and Dumont Streets, which she remembered passing three blocks away.

She left the house and briskly walked back to Dumont Street. She waited about ten minutes before the cab arrived. She hopped in and told him she wanted to go to the Alamo.

She had considered staying at Senator Marshall's but discarded the idea. The family could return at any time.

Perhaps she could stay in a busy hotel, but how could she check in without using a credit card? It would be too easy for Jim to trace either her cards or his American Express.

She'd rather sleep in a sewer than risk having Jim learn her whereabouts.

That was her thinking when she left the senator's house, but by the time she had taken her stroll on the *Paseo del Rio,* she knew she had to call Mike Talamino.

Chapter 13

Mike had listened to her story, rarely interjecting any comments. He simply nodded, furrowed his brow at places, smiled at others. When she finished, he prodded her with questions. His memory was uncanny. He remembered every detail she had uttered.

She had told him that Jim and his cohorts might have found out about him by now from the letter, but she hoped the false name had thrown them.

"That's a possibility since I live in an apartment complex," he said. "They could think that Mike Q. Public had moved or that you wrote down the wrong apartment number, but I'm afraid it's only a matter of time before they find out I used to live in Austin or learn of my former connection with you."

He got up and stretched, then walked over to the French windows. He looked at the river for a few minutes before turning back to her. "Do you have any idea when Senator Marshall plans to return to San Antonio?

Lacy shrugged.

Biting his lip, he strolled back to her bed and sat on it. "You never had any suspicions until your trip to Schneiderburg?"

She shook her head.

"I want you to think hard now, try to think of anything before then which did not at the time seem questionable but under the light of what you now know might be."

Lacy sat silent for several minutes. At last her face alighted as if she had just recognized a once-cherished friend. "I know how we can get the...Well, I'm not exactly sure, but I'm almost certain--"

"Get to the point."

"It's McNally's files. I always thought they contained data on contributors, but from the way he guards those things now I believe they might conceal details of their shady transactions or maybe even blackmail information against senators. He keeps them in his office under lock and key. No one else, absolutely no one, ever gets near that filing cabinet.

"Where does he keep the key?"

"In the locked top drawer of his desk."

"You've got no evidence which would be admissible in court," he said.

"The men in the blue car were the likely murderers of Mr. Bryson, and I can establish a connection between myself and him and say that the men followed me."

He smoothed her rich brown hair away

from her face. "We need evidence that doesn't hinge on your testimony. On the evidence we've got right now it wouldn't be too wise to bust this thing wide open. Somehow, without endangering you any more, we've got to dig up more evidence.

"Why don't I just walk into Jim's office with a concealed tape recorder?"

"I was thinking about those files in McNally's office. I bet they're loaded with incriminating evidence, probably enough to hang the whole lot of them. But how can we get our hands on them?"

"You're either crazy or you don't know the security system at the Capitol."

"Do you know much about it?"

"Not really. I know they have closed-circuit television cameras all over the place, but I don't know where. There's one guard at the monitoring station around the clock. That station is in the open on the ground floor."

"Have you ever been at the Capitol late at night?"

"Many times."

"Tell me everything you know about the security system at that hour."

"Well, I've never really thought about it before. Let's see... There's one guy who stays at the TV screens. There's usually three or four guards standing around near there. They have walkie-talkies. The whole lot of them generally appear to be engaged in conversation. I've never seen them in any other part of the Capitol at that hour. I've seen maybe one or two guards circling the exterior of the building in a small mobile unit, too." She paused for several seconds, then added, "That's really about all I know."

He sat silently, deeply intent on his own thoughts. Finally, with a grave look, he spoke. "Do you think you could sneak in there tomorrow night?"

At first she thought he had been kidding, but then she realized he was serious. She had just begun to relax all over. She had thought now that Mike was here she could wake up from her bad dream just as she had done when she was a child. As soon as she was by her mother's side, everything was all right. That's how she had felt all evening. Mike was here. He'd take care of everything.

But now she realized her part in the nightmare was not over. With or without Mike she would have to finish. "I suppose I can't be in much more danger than I've already faced, and it might furnish the lucky break we need." Deep concern crossed her face. "But, Mike, are you sure you want to risk your life for it?"

"Don't forget I'm a champion of justice." He winked. "Actually, much of my work lately has been of the investigative nature. Of course in this case we don't just go into the Capitol, flash our ID and get all the answers.

I'm afraid all we'd get would be a bullet in the back."

"That seems a certainty."

"I'm not going to put all of our eggs into the same basket, though. I'm going to try to get a lead on those guys in the blue car. We do know one of them is named Pete, and you can give a good description of him. I know quite a few FBI investigators. Surely I'll know one of the ones on the case."

He looked at his watch, then jumped up and turned on the television, in time to be greeted by the local news commentator.

"I want to see if they have anything about you on the news." They watched until the first commercial. The only news about Lacy was the wedding announcement. A still photo of Lacy flashed across the screen.

"My, but you're quite a celebrity."

"Oh, shut up," she said, flashing a white-toothed smile.

"At least Chambers is running too scared to throw around his power in his search for you. I would have thought he'd have an APB out for you by now. I'm sure, though, that he'll have his private network of thugs out in full force. Luckily for us, until they find the car they'll probably think you're still in Austin." They watched the remainder of the newscast, relieved to find out that she was not being hunted publicly. She would not have been surprised to learn that every policeman in the state was hunting her. Jim had said he was in the process of framing her for some loathsome crime.

"One of the FBI agents here in San Antonio is a friend of mine—we went to school together. I'm going to call him from a pay phone and find out who's on the case in Austin. I should be back within an hour." He paused. "If I'm not, get in touch with Eddie Wickland, the one I'm calling now."

After he left she took a steaming shower, then put on her Alamo T-shirt and crawled into bed, leaving the bedside light on.

A compulsive reader, she picked up the phone book and read the columns on places of interest in San Antonio, studied the sketchy map and was thumbing through the yellow pages when she heard someone put the key card into the door. She put her hand on the phone, thinking she might have time to call for help if the intruder was not Mike.

It was Mike. She sank back to a reclining position.

"I got ahold of Eddie's wife." He came and sat on the side of her bed. "She said he'd been assigned to the Austin case and was staying at the Hilton there, so I called him—told him I might have some information on his case, but that I couldn't tell him yet because my informant's life was in danger. I asked what leads he had, and he said he still had nothing on the guys in the blue car. Their only lead is that Bryson had asked the local police for information on the cop who was killed by a sniper, the one who investigated Ruth Chambers' fatal accident."

Lacy sat up and ran a finger across the stubble on his cheek. "You look tired."

He got to his feet. "I am." He hadn't met her gaze. "Think I'll shut off the light, take off my clothes, and get some shut-eye."

As she lay in the darkness, she heard his pants unzip and fall to the floor, then he was picking them up. He must be flattening them out so he won't lose his creases, she thought. He took a few steps. She knew he was hanging them over the back of the chair. Then she heard him get into the room's other full-size bed.

After a few minutes, he called her name into the darkness.

"Huh?" she answered.

"Why did you turn to me after these two years without a word?"

"I've been thinking about you a lot lately. I sort of unconsciously realized recently that I was pretty foolish two years ago." She had to change the subject or she'd spill out her guts. And she couldn't throw herself at him. She had her pride.

Maybe she could handle the situation more lightly. "I met a friend of yours at a party a couple of weeks ago," she said. "I don't remember his name, but he worked with you in Houston. I took care to ask him if you were married." She had gone as far as she dared. The next move had to be his. She almost held her breath.

The ensuing silence provoked her. If only he would speak. After a while he said, "I haven't found the girl who could knock you off the pedestal I placed you on." He said it without assurance, a funny little catch in his normally strident voice.

But the words were more tender than any proclamation of love could ever have been. What could she ever have done to merit such ecstasy? "Oh, Mike, that's the nicest thing anyone ever said to me."

Though they were separated by four or five feet, she had never felt so close to him before.

After a minute of thoughtful silence, she continued. "I don't understand myself. Never before or since have I cared for anyone the way I cared for you. Why didn't I ever tell you? And, why didn't you ever tell me? Never did I know for sure that you..."

"That I loved you?"

Her heart soared.

"I didn't think I had to tell you. I shared every day with you for twenty-six months. No two people could have been closer."

"But, Mike, never did you tell me you loved me. Never did you speak of our future. I never knew I was anything more than a close friend—albeit one with whom you were physically intimate." The very memory of making love with him sent her heartbeat hammering.

He laughed. A bitter laugh. "I've chided myself thousands of times since then for not telling you. But you got in the way of my master plan. I wasn't supposed to fall in love until I had five years of legal practice under my belt. I didn't want wife and family getting in the way of my career. I tried to ignore my emotions. It was stupid of me."

How could anyone facing the danger she was in feel anything like bliss, but that is what the very idea of marrying him evoked.

It was funny that now in the total darkness he could tell her things he could never say face to face.

"I thought it was hopeless," she continued. "I was unhappy over our relationship, unhappy that it was going nowhere at the time of our...our breakup. That was so foolish for us to fight over Jim of all things. When you got transferred to Houston, I thought that'd be a good time to try to forget about you."

"And I thought I could forget about you," he said, his voice low and gentle.

To hell with her pride. The only thing on this earth that mattered now was Mike. Mike who was risking his life for her. God, she loved him. Never had it ever been anyone but Mike.

And she was going to show him how much.

She slipped from her bed and moved to him. He scooted over to make room for her beside him as he drew her to him. She nestled her face in the soft hair of his chest, basking in the comfort of him, sliding her hands over his bare, muscled back. His lips hungrily sought hers. His hands and mouth were gentle and arousing.

He made love to her. Slow and tender and agonizing in its intensity. When they finished, he held her close. Like everything he'd done that night, it was a protective gesture. He hadn't spoken his feelings. He showed them.

Before long, he drifted off to sleep, his warm flesh melding with hers. She lay awake long afterward. She scarcely thought of the danger they faced. Instead, she thought of this man who lay so close to her, of how very much in love with him she was. She drew in the musky, masculine scent of this most beloved man, listened to his reassuring breathing, and stroked his sinewy body.

Chapter 14

Lacy woke up to the thud of a door swiftly closing. She sprang up in time to see Mike place a breakfast tray on the dresser near the door. He turned and saw her.

She suddenly became conscious of her nakedness and pulled up the sheets.

"My, but you slept well. It's almost eleven. I've been up an hour already. I went down to the haberdashery and picked up a new shirt and pants and something for you."

"Haberdashery? I didn't know anyone said that nowadays." She grinned.

He shrugged. "I guess that does sound corny." He peered at her, devilment in his dark eyes. "You gotta remember my dad was very old when I was born. He always called men's clothiers haberdasheries."

He pulled a baseball-style cap from his bag and handed it to her.

"Never let me say you aren't romantic," she said dryly.

"It's to help disguise you." He took off his shirt. "Here, put this on. I can't seem to concentrate on anything when you're sitting there like that." He gave it to her, then turned around to busy himself with the breakfast tray.

Seeing him without a shirt—lean and hard and dark—made it hard for her to concentrate on anything except him. She put the shirt and cap on, still letting the sheets cover up the lower part of her body.

"This morning you're going to be served breakfast in bed. It's just one of the little extras that come with my services."

"You are so very dear," she said softly. Her eyes dropped to the tray he was bringing. "What did you order?"

"Coffee. Orange juice. Bacon and eggs. And toast. How does that suit her majesty?"

"Fantastic."

He sat beside her with the tray between them. She poured coffee from the Pyrex decanter into her cup. He devoured two eggs, four slices of bacon and one piece of toast in less than five minutes.

"Have you thought any more about what we'll do?" she asked.

"Yes, I think I've about got everything worked out. Our biggest obstacle is transportation—how we can get back to Austin without being caught. Chambers is bound to have someone at the airports and bus stations, and he's probably got someone checking all the car rental places in this part of the state. Becky's car, of course, is absolutely out."

"That's a pretty bleak picture you're painting."

He got up and put the tray on the dresser. "I think I should be able to hot wire that car of Senator Marshall's that was in his garage yesterday when you dumped Becky's there. I'll first need to find out if he or a member of his family plans on returning to San Antonio any time soon. I'll go find a phone booth and call his Austin hotel with some phony story."

She could think of nothing but her separation from Mike. "Why can't I go with you?"

"There's an outside chance of your being recognized, even with a disguise." He came to sit on her bed and gently traced the contours of her face with a single finger. She inched closer to him until their lips met. She melted into him as his arms closed around her.

Suddenly, he stood up. "First things first, Lacy. We've got to get this mess straightened out before we can count on being alive next week."

He walked to the dresser and picked up a couple of magazines Lacy had not noticed before. "I got these for you to read while I'm traipsing around today. See, I remembered what an omnivorous reader you are." A wide smile flashed over his face. "Just another of my little services."

She masked her disappointment. "I

appreciate you. How could I have ever let you out of my life?"

He walked back and lifted her chin, a slow smile lighting his somber face. "When the maid comes, tell her you just want towels. Don't let her in," he commanded. "And if you get to feeling isolated, you can go out on the balcony as long as you've got on a hat."

"Yes, sir,"

"I won't be more than a couple of hours," he told her as he left.

After dressing, she plopped on the bed and thumbed through the magazines, but her mind wandered. Since Mike had rescued her the night before, she no longer felt the burdensome weight of their dangerous situation. It was as if he had completely shouldered her load, leaving her in his protective care. She resented it none. Letting Mike Talamino take care of her was what she had wanted all her life. The deadly threat Jim Chambers posed for her did not cross her mind. Instead, she worried about Mike's feeling for her. Did he truly love her? Would he want to take care of her for the rest of her life?

Then, she wondered if the two of them would be alive next week.

Now, she wanted to think of something more pleasant.

Mike. Always it would be Mike. It was foolish, she told herself, to sit there worrying over whether Mike loved her when death loomed so near. She earnestly tried to find an article in the magazine which might help her escape from her thoughts. She wasn't interested in the fashion advertisements today, although she usually was. She wanted to become absorbed in something remote. Ironically, an article on new trends in day care centers attracted her. Her first impulse was that she had to clip the story for her files. Then she remembered she would never again use those files.

She read the story, nevertheless, and it brought her back to the consciousness of her shaky existence by reminding her of the would-be day care center in Schneiderburg.

She put the magazine down and vowed the children of Schneiderburg would get their day care center.

Worrying about Mike was taking its toll on her nerves. She decided to take his advice and gaze over the gala town from her balcony perch. She walked to the French windows and opened one before she remembered that she was not wearing a hat. She went back in and put it on, returning to the balcony.

Lacy sat hypnotized over the Alamo City. Everywhere she looked she saw happiness and love. There must have been loners in the thick masses below her, but these she did not notice. As she had the night before, she noted with interest dozens of young servicemen, their arms tucked around their girls, broad smiles covering their faces. More of the same smiling faces on those riverboats crammed with tourists.

A large family strolling the River Walk below caught her eye. She knew it must be a family, for the children were stair steps of one another. The proud Hispanic parents each carried a baby. Lacy counted six children. Although their clothes were ill fit and unstylish, they were clean. And as children the world over do, they were exploding with excitement over what was obviously a very special family outing. The young mother kept rebuking the two oldest boys for stepping dangerously close to the river's edge.

The images below only made her more conscious of how alone she was without this man who had been gone less than two hours. She looked at her watch. It was two. He would be back soon, she thought. She went back into the room to put on her makeup to look her best for his return.

Afterwards, she waited. Two thirty. Three o'clock. Three thirty came and still no Mike. The maid had come and gone without seeing Lacy's face, leaving only towels at Lacy's request.

Lacy started to worry. He'd been gone three hours already. She tried again to get interested in the slick pages of the magazine, but couldn't. Her hands were shaking. Then it was four and still no word from him.

When five came and she had not heard from him, she was not just edgy; she was terrified. He had said he wouldn't be more than a couple of hours, and already it had been four and a half. A dreadful suspicion kept pushing its way into her thoughts. She fought it, but it kept creeping back, telling her Jim Chambers had learned where she ditched the car, and he had laid a trap for Mike at Senator Marshall's house. Agony and sheer terror nearly paralyzed her.

Chapter 15

Several times she lifted the phone receiver only to put it back down, quickly realizing that no one could help. *One way or another, I'll hear something*, she thought anxiously.

What she heard was the entry card slipping into their hotel room door. She caught her breath.

And saw Mike stroll into the room.

She ran and hurled herself into him. "I've been insane with worry."

He set his hands firmly on her shoulders. "Everything's okay. Let's sit down, and I'll tell you what happened."

He had called Senator Marshall's office, he told her, explaining that he was calling from the San Antonio Chamber of Commerce. He told the senator the chamber was initiating a series of banquets honoring public officials. The first, which they hoped he could attend as the honored guest, would be the coming Saturday, followed by another in four weeks. He asked the senator which of the dates would be more satisfactory. The senator replied that he was snowed under with committee hearings through the current week and would not be able to get back to San Antonio that early, and his family was spending the coming weekend in Mexico.

"All right!" Lacy exclaimed.

"Then I went to his house so I could get the car. Unfortunately, as soon as I had snuck into the garage through the back door, I heard someone pull up in the driveway. It was the yard man. It took him three hours to do the front and back yards."

She ran her hand along his cheek. "You're here now."

"By the way, I want you to put this in your purse. It's precharged." From a grocery sack he had brought he held up a cordless drill. "If it won't fit, we'll get you a bigger purse. We may not be able to get into McNally's files tonight without that little gem. Someday, I hope to give thanks to Senator Marshall."

Lacy examined it. "If I leave out a few things, I think I can fit it in my purse."

He nodded. "While you spent the afternoon reading in a nice, air-conditioned hotel room, I lurked in a dark pantry which smelled of stale crackers."

"I was terrified all afternoon," she chided. "I imagined all sorts of terrible things had happened to you." The scolding tone of her voice gave way to softness. "I'm glad you're back in one piece." She wished she weren't so transparent. He knew exactly how she felt, yet he erected a barrier to his own feelings.

"We've got plans to make before we embark on..." He stopped short.

He had started to say something more but held it back. He was worried, Lacy knew, about what lay ahead that evening. She also knew that he wouldn't tell her his fears.

"First," he continued, "let's get a good meal. We can face anything with a good meal under our belts. I'll order dinner from room service, and we'll sit on the balcony."

"Food is not the world's cure-all. I believe if you were a condemned man your last request would be for some of Mama's ravioli."

He laughed. "You remembered." He took a menu out of the bureau drawer and scanned it. "Looks like I'll have to settle for lobster." He handed the menu to Lacy. "What would you like?"

Lacy waved off the menu. "I'll have whatever you're having."

"And wouldn't a bottle of Pinot Grigio go well with it?"

She nodded. "I haven't had Italian wine in two years."

He called in the order.

When the food arrived, Lacy went into the bathroom while the waiter set up a card table on the balcony. After helping to set table, the waiter left. Lacy took one last look in the mirror before coming out. She had donned the baseball cap Mike had bought her that morning. Too bad she wouldn't look sexy.

Mike scarcely looked up at her. He was lifting the silver covers off the plates. "Doesn't this look great?"

Lacy pulled out her own chair and sat down.

He proceeded to shell the lobsters, without saying anything. "Go ahead and start eating," he finally told her.

After their plates were filled, he uncorked the wine, poured out two glasses, and handed one to Lacy.

By now she had stopped looking at him. The rustle of nearby treetops diverted her. She looked down at them, a mixture of the local greens: palms, mesquite and oak.

"It's really lovely here," she said. "And this is the perfect time to enjoy a meal on the balcony. Twilight. You can still enjoy the view, yet you don't have to bear the day's heat."

"Yes, everything's perfect." He reached for her hand. They sat silently for a few minutes. They were much closer now than they ever bad been.

He spoke first. "I can't help but think of Omar Khayyam. 'A jug of wine, a loaf of bread—and thou.'"

He looked into Lacy's eyes. "And like the narrator of the poem, I want to take what I can from this short life." He recited by memory:

Ah, make the most of what we yet may spend,
Before we too into the Dust descend,
Dust into Dust, and under Dust to lie,
Sans Wine, Sans Song, Sans Singer, and sans End.

After a moment's silence, Lacy said, "Beautiful, but a bit morbid. Since you're in a poetic mood, why don't you quote something more joyful?"

"There's always an end to joy, hence sadness."

"I suppose you're right." She nodded slowly, squeezing his hand. She didn't like the moroseness. Was it a portent?

They ate in a comfortable silence.

"Michael Talamino, you know you're quite a paradox. On the one hand you're completely aloof—romantically. And on the other you recite poetry like a lovelorn spinster."

"You look beautiful," he interrupted.

It was all he said, yet he had said much more.

After the meal they cleared away the table, but remained on the balcony until twilight faded into darkness. They felt very close, sitting there holding hands. After what could have been an hour, perhaps more, perhaps less, he said, "I hate to bring us out of this . . . this comfort zone, but it's time we make preparations for our...our late-night mission."

The curtain was drawn again. It was not what she had hoped he would say, yet it was typical of him. Always the practical one. "I'm sure you must have a well-planned scheme brewing. Let's have it."

"Well, I do have a scheme, but it's certainly not elaborate. As a matter of fact, it's so corny I think it might work, but I don't need to tell you now. That can wait till we're in the car."

"Oh, the car. Did you have any problems with it?"

"That was the only easy thing all afternoon. In a little porcelain box on the countertop between the kitchen and the garage I found the key to the BMW convertible. "

"I'm glad *one* thing worked out so well."

A moment later, a look of concern crossed his face. "You don't have to go tonight. I have to."

"Silly thing, I got you into this, and I'm not about to let you hang yourself with my rope. Absolutely nothing could keep me away from there tonight. Where's the car?"

"A couple of blocks from here in a parking garage. Things there seemed so efficiently automated that I felt the human attendants wouldn't notice people."

"Ver-r-r-ry clever." She had been stuffing her few possessions into the suitcase. Before closing the suitcase she dumped in everything from her large, hobo-style leather purse, then she jammed the bulky drill into her bag.

Her arm nearly gave under the unexpected weight of the drill in her purse. As they neared the door, Lacy turned back and gave the room a last look. "I've been happy here," she told him.

He smiled down at her. "We'll come back sometime."

God, but she hoped he was right.

They were stepping off the elevator in the lobby when Lacy saw the back of a familiar-looking redhead at the desk. Her fingers dug into Mike's arm, her pulse pounded with fear.

"What's wrong?"

"That red-headed man over at the desk...I think he's the one," she whispered, her voice uneven.

"Good God, don't let him see you!" He was trying now to shield her with his body from the redhead's line of vision. Mike glanced around the lobby "You need to get the hell out of here." He walked her to the door leading to the *Paseo del Rio,* shielding her body from the redhead's sight. "Wait for me on the River Walk near the hump-back bridge."

She nearly ran. She wanted to get as far away from the hotel and Pete as she could. *He's my assassin* she kept telling herself. Jim had sent him to kill her.

She prayed for Mike's safety as she crossed the bridge. She would wait for him on the other side of the river.

The wait seemed hideously long. When she finally saw Mike exit the hotel and begin to walk toward the bridge, she walked to meet him half way, relief pulsing through her veins. "Well?" she asked.

He sighed. "It was him. He was flashing around your photo and trying to bribe the desk clerk. He offered him fifty bucks to let him see the names of those who checked in during the last day."

She winced.

"If I hadn't been standing there, I'm sure the guy would have taken the fifty."

"Oh, my god! How did they find out I was in San Antonio?"

"By tracking me. The guy had my name."

"So they checked airlines and found out you bought a ticket to San Antonio last night?"

He nodded. "Apparently." He led her to the street level. "We're getting the hell out of here."

"Where to?"

"We're going to visit the Capitol building."

Chapter 16

Night was straining to replace twilight. Any of the tall surrounding buildings could be hiding the stealthy redhead at this very minute. The eeriness of the darkened streets frightened Lacy. She kept telling herself that each slap of their shoes against the pavement placed them another step away from her assassin. She would not feel safe until they reached the parking garage.

When Mike finally turned into the parking garage, she let out a little sigh.

They drove in silence. Once out of the city limits, they still did not speak of what they both wanted to discuss—their trip to Austin and his plan of action.

Few cars were on the road. The poor lighting and sparsely populated terrain only contributed to Lacy's anxiety. Under the stark glow of oncoming headlights, the roadside trees had about them a ghost-like quality that gave Lacy the sensation of having stumbled into a nightmarish neverland.

Sensing her distress, Mike turned the radio on to a San Antonio rock station. The loud tunes with their deep bass beat seemed to lift her spirits. She patted his muscular thigh to let him know she was all right.

"We'd better talk." He smiled and turned off the radio. "Remember when I told you my plan for gaining access to the Capitol without alarming the security guards was pretty corny?"

"Um huh."

"Well, here's the gist of it. We'll park the car right off the Capitol grounds. Does the building still stay open until ten?'

"Yep."

"We can't risk them recognizing the senator's car. We also can't risk them recognizing you. Stick your hair up in a pony tail and smash that baseball cap I got you on your head. We need to play the tourist bit, taking a romantic stroll through the hallowed halls. We walk in arm-in-arm, careful that they don't get a look at your face. We'll look at the statues and pictures and all. Then we'll scan the newsstand near the guards' station. That's where it will happen."

"What?"

"That's where I'm going to feign a heart attack."

"Oh, brother."

"I know it sound crazy and risky, but I think there's a pretty good chance of it working. Do you have any aspirins in your purse?"

"Yes. Do you need one?"

"Not now. At the Capitol."

"I'm afraid you've confounded me terribly."

"I suppose I have. I need the aspirins for when I fake the attack. You're supposed to say you have to run to the car for my nitroglycerin pills. You'll substitute aspirins for nitro. Instead of going to the car, though, you go to McNally's office. Hopefully, the guy who monitors the closed circuit television will have come to our rescue so you'll have a clear time of it. You've got the key to McNally's office?"

"Yes. To where his secretaries receive people."

"Can you get the key to his office from his secretary's desk drawer and let yourself into his office?"

"Just one problem. His desk is always locked."

"In the course of my duties, I've learned a little about lock picking," he said with exaggeration.

"All right, Houdini."

"Actually, I was kidding. I know nothing of lock picking, but I think the drill might do the trick. You drill out the portion of wood which surrounds the lock on the top middle drawer."

After a few minutes she said, "You know, I think your crazy plan might work...There is one possible problem."

"Which is?"

"You know the lieutenant governor has living chambers there?"

"In the Capitol?"

"Yep. On the Senate side of the building, near his staff's offices."

"Do you know if he'll be in tonight?"

"I have no idea."

"We'll have to take our chances." He switched the radio back on and continued driving fast. The speedometer reached eighty. "I'd like to make it before ten."

"Don't go past eighty, please. You don't want to get stopped for speeding. It might prove embarrassing with a stolen car."

"Yes, ma'am."

In spite of Mike's jovial facade, she still worried about their mission. "Mike, what will we do with the evidence—if we get it tonight?"

"I'll turn it over to my friends in the FBI. Once I've got evidence, I don't mind making a big stir. But you know from your own experience, you don't make waves until you put the culprits behind bars. And only tangible evidence can do that."

With plenty of time to spare before ten, they saw the lighted dome of the Capitol building. It was another twenty minutes, however, before they neared the Capitol grounds.

Chapter 17

Things went as Mike had predicted. They parked at the foot of the Capitol, not on the grounds but on Congress Avenue. The downtown area was deserted but well lit. Hand in hand, they walked up the landscaped grounds, the golden glow of the capitol's lighted dome arched against the black sky. Wearing baggy jeans, reading glasses, the Alamo T-shirt, and baseball cap, Lacy began to shiver. Mike put his arm around her.

Together, they mounted the granite steps and passed through the huge doors. Though Lacy had been here at night countless times, it was like she was seeing the magnificent building for the first time. She and Mike seemed so insignificant. Mere specks of dust on the dimly lit terrazzo hallways that were here a century and a half ago and would be here the next century. They stopped to look at massive portraits, Lacy careful to use Mike's body to shield her face from view of anyone who might happen in.

The voices of the guards in the next room

echoed in the towering halls. Apparently Mike and Lacy had been dismissed as tourists. Arm in arm, they browsed through history's memorabilia, coming at last to a halt at the newsstands which displayed the state's major daily newspapers as well as the principle weeklies.

When three guards left the monitoring station to check the halls, Mike grabbed at his chest.

Lacy shrieked and darted toward him as he crouched to the floor. She fell to her knees beside him.

Just as Mike had anticipated, the man monitoring the screens left his station to give aid to Mike. Within seconds, several guards surrounded the crouched couple.

"Honey, where are your pills?" Lacy asked. Then she screamed out, "Oh, my God, they're in the car." She sprang to her feet and ran off, calling over her shoulder, "I'll be right back with the pills. Hold on."

Off she ran. Only, she turned, and with speed she never knew she had, ran up the stairs, and down the darkened halls to McNally's office without encountering anyone.

Quickly, she took the key from her purse, unlocked the massive door, and stepped in. Groping in total darkness, she managed, with the aid of a mental picture firmly impressed on her brain from hundreds of visits here, to find Vera's desk. She fingered its smooth oak.

The drawer was not locked and opened easily. Fumbling, she found the key to McNally's office.

Still stepping cautiously in the dark, she guided herself to where she thought the door to McNally's office was. Blank wall. Sliding against the wall, taking it slowly, she soon came to the door and inserted the key into the lock. It opened with no trouble.

This room was lighted from the generous windows. She approached the desk and tried the top drawer on the off chance that McNally had left it unlocked. It was locked. She would have to use the drill.

Before turning it on, her stomach knotted. She knew a certain amount of noise would accompany the drilling, but, weighing the odds again, felt her chances of survival would be greater with Jim Chambers behind bars. And she hoped she was going to find evidence that would guarantee her safety. Without it, she was dead meat.

With sweating hands, she turned it on and quickly bore away a v-shaped wedge on the portion of the drawer surrounding the lock. The wedge slipped away in a few seconds, and the drawer freely slid back and forth.

Lacy felt for the key. Luck was with her still. It, too, was there. Eagerly, she opened up the top drawer of the filing cabinet. Like most filing cabinets, it was alphabetically indexed, starting with the A's. She knew she was racing against time and wouldn't have all night to browse through the files looking for just the right bit of incriminating evidence.

She quickly thought of a once-liberal, vituperative state senator, Al Simpson, who, two years earlier, reversed his opposition to Jim Chambers and began rubberstamping all of Chambers' endorsements. Lacy had wondered why he had changed so completely, so suddenly. Now, she might find out. She opened up the R through V drawer. Under the S's she did, indeed, find a file on Al Simpson. She grabbed up the manila folder. In it, among other things, was a Xeroxed club roster, some twenty years old. Simpson had signed it while he was a student at Texas Tech. The club was titled Student Religious Liberals. He had signed "Al Simpson, devout atheist."

"So," thought Lacy, Jim *was* blackmailing him. Simpson knew his rural constituents would never re-elect a man they thought was an atheist.

She kept out the file and quickly snatched others. At random, she looked under the R's. Myron Rainey, the imminent state supreme court justice, merited his own file. In his folder Lacy saw, but did not look at too closely, a photograph of the elderly judge in bed with a young woman who most definitely was not Mrs. Rainey. Hating to do it, she kept out this file, too.

Turning back to the top drawer, she looked under day care. It seemed unbelievable to Lacy, but there was actually a file on the shady transactions at the Schneiderburg day care center. Deeds and canceled checks and even a payroll to nonexistent day care workers.

Just as she was about to put the files in her purse, she heard the outer office door open.

Her insides jolted violently. Sweat drenched her. Her first instinct of survival was to hide. But where? The desk was the only shelter in the room, and it was of little help. She edged up against the wall, wedged between the filing cabinet and the window. She would be hidden for a few seconds, but if someone were looking for her, they would find her easily.

She shook all over and was afraid to breathe for fear of being heard. She heard footsteps coming across the receiving office. Then she heard McNally's door open—she'd forgotten to relock it. She childishly hoped it was just a watchman making his rounds, or even McNally, hurriedly fetching something from his desktop. Perhaps, she tried to assure herself, whoever it was would just turn around and go away.

The overhead light flashed on. Footsteps came toward her. She knew the top of her was lower than the top of the filing cabinet because she stooped at the knees, but she suddenly discovered that since the light had been turned on, her reflection showed in the nearby window, just as Jim's did as he came toward her.

"Hello, Lacy."

She looked up and saw the gleam of the gun he pointed at her.

Her first sensation was of total fear. After a few seconds, though, her logically calculating mind took charge, giving her renewed strength. "Jim, you couldn't possibly use that gun in this building. Not even you could get away with that."

"Don't be so certain. I don't want to use the gun in this building, but I will if I have to. I've already figured out my story. I'll say I was alarmed by the twisting of my outer door knob as I was up late reading. I got up to investigate, just in time to see a short man with a hat enter McNally's office. And knowing it couldn't be McNally, I got my gun and came upon the intruder who was stealing from McNally's cash reserve. There was a struggle, of course, and the gun went off."

"They'll never believe you."

"I think they will."

"How did you know someone was in here?"

"I heard a sound like a drill. You know, only that wall there separates my bedroom from Richard's office. Instinct told me it was either you or that Italian fellow of yours. Naturally, I came to investigate."

"How'd you find out about Mike?"

"From your letter, of course. One of my men in Houston followed up my lead. It seems a Mike Talamino, rather than a Mike Q. Public, lived at the address, and after some investigation we determined that Mike Talamino had not shown up at work today— very out of character, according to his co-workers. The fact he graduated from UT law school placed him in Austin, so it seemed likely you and he had known each other. From the Houston airport my man was able to find out that Talamino had gone to San Antonio the night before. How, I'm wondering, did you make it through my usually capable network in San Antonio?"

"Let your usually capable network figure that out."

"Where's the boyfriend?"

Lacy looked at her watch. "If I'm not out of here in five minutes, he'll bring the FBI after you."

"I'm not going to fall for that. My men will be able to deal with him. Now, I want to escort you into my apartment until I decide how to dispose of you. I hope I don't have to remind you not to try to escape. I'm quite a good shot." Thinking of Mike, Lacy's confidence suddenly buoyed, so sure she was of his ability to get her out of this perilous situation.

She and Jim walked the short distance

from McNally's office to Jim's spacious lieutenant governor's apartment.

He led her to his study and ordered her to take a seat in a straight chair near the desk. With his gun still aimed at her, he lifted the phone receiver and punched a number.

"Rich, Lacy's here with me. I caught her breaking into your files. Can you come over right away?" He watched Lacy as he listened.

After he hung up, he punched out another number, this one only four digits—indicating that he was calling someone in the Capitol complex.

"Bernie," he began, "this is Lieutenant Governor Chambers. Has a young, dark man been hanging around down there?" Another pause, this one longer. Instead of replying, Jim broke into laughter. "Well, I'd rather that we'd have gotten him first, but I guess it's too late now. How'd you like to earn ten thousand dollars? Here's what you do. Try to keep the fellow from contacting anyone. You grab him as soon as he posts bail. I don't care what you have to do. Pete ought to be back in time to help you take care of him once you've got him."

With a sadistic smile of his face, Jim glared at Lacy. "Now I know how you and the boyfriend got past my men in San Antonio. We'd covered the car rental agencies, airport, bus and train stations. Pity we didn't post someone at Senator Marshall's unoccupied house. By the way, the Senator was working late and just happened to drive by just as you and Talamino left the little sports car. He immediately confirmed that it was his car, watched the pair of you enter the Capitol, then called the Capitol police to report it."

At least Jim didn't have Mike yet, Lacy assured herself. But, it was of little comfort, knowing the strong forces that worked against them. She decided to find out more about those forces.

"What do you mean by your network? Do you actually have some sort of crime ring under your command?"

"I guess you could call it that. Sort of a miniature mafia. I'm at the head of it—started laying the foundation for it when I was still a state rep. Small stuff at first. A little blackmail here, securing state contracts for various business associates of mine. When I became lieutenant governor we really got organized. Me, Richard, the Schneiderburg realtor, and big businessmen from around the state. We've got a payroll of over a hundred. You might call it my own private army."

"Oh, God, you sound mentally deranged."

"Is that why you didn't fall for me?"

"I've only recently learned of your problem."

"I could tell you always thought you were too good for me. You and that ultra-respectable family of yours. All the money I've got couldn't buy you. I would have bought you everything you could ever have wanted if you'd just have married me. There's not a woman in this whole building who wouldn't go to bed with me without a minute's hesitation. Don't look at me so high and mighty."

"I'm not looking any particular way at you."

"You damned bitch. Not everyone had the advantages you had. Do you know what it is to work two jobs and rob your sleep in order to study to get through college? I used to wash dishes at the girls' dorm for my meals. It was not only humiliating, it was also slave's work in that steaming kitchen."

"You can cut out the Horatio Alger stories, Jim. On a professor's salary, my dad couldn't afford to send all of us to school. We got some help with scholarships, but we all worked."

The door to McNally's office burst open.

Chapter 18

"I let myself in," McNally told Chambers.

"Glad you got here so fast." Jim did not take his eyes off Lacy nor his finger off the trigger of the gun. "We've got to get her out of here right away. There's an outside chance that boyfriend of hers may be able to get someone to search my place when he can't find her. He's being booked right now for car theft, but he may be able to get someone to listen to him. Bernie's going to try to hit him as soon as he's out."

Lacy's heart stilled.

"Better get her out of here fast," McNally said.

"Can you take her to your place?" Jim asked.

McNally shook his head. "What would I tell Viv?"

Now Lacy was absolutely certain Vivian McNally was completely ignorant of her husband's crimes.

"Better not put a blabbing female to the test," Jim said. "Before we do another thing, I want you to call the guys in San Antonio and tell 'em to cool it because they're here, and tell 'em to send Pete back right away."

McNally punched a phone number and dittoed his boss's instructions, then hung up. "As good as done. Now, about our problem...What do you think about me taking her to mine and Viv's bay house while you fix things up here? You can send Pete down later. I could get there in about four hours and could be back by noon tomorrow—if you send Pete on."

Lacy knew Pete would be her assassin. And a guy named Bernie, Mike's. As terrified as she was, she was sick that she'd involved Mike, sick that because he loved her, he, too, would die.

"Sounds good."

"Let me call Viv before I take off."

So she would be carried off to an out-of-season bay home where Pete would murder her. Tears surged. Her heartbeat thundered. They spoke of getting rid of her as if she were just so much waste which had to be disposed of. If only there were some way she could get a message out.

Then, it occurred to her. In their anxiety, McNally and Jim were nearly unaware of the threat of her presence. When McNally called his wife, Lacy could make her move if she acted quickly enough.

She was ready after he had punched in the phone number. At the precise second he said *hello,* Lacy screamed out: "Help Lacy, Vivian!"

McNally slammed down the phone, then slapped Lacy. The force knocked her to the floor. She was almost glad of his sudden blow because she had been afraid that in his anger Jim might have pulled the trigger. Now, he could be cooling off while she dragged herself off the floor.

The surprise and sting of the attack had brought tears streaming down her face. Jim jerked her off the floor and clenched his hand over her mouth while the other hand held her arm. Unmasked evil shone in his face. "We'd better tie and gag her."

McNally nodded. "But what will I tell Viv? I'm afraid she'll call back any second."

He was no longer the wise administrator. Now he was a scared man begging instructions.

Jim swept up the phone receiver and placed it on the desk.

"There. If she calls back, she'll think we're on the phone. And turn off your goddamn cell phone, too."

"She knows she heard her name called out," McNally protested.

"I doubt if she can be sure it was you who placed the call. Remember, you didn't say anything but 'hi.' I'll leave the phone off the hook until we can plan on what to tell her. She wouldn't call the police without getting in touch with you first."

"Let me be responsible for Viv," McNally pleaded. "Don't do anything that'll hurt her." He looked worried. His hand wiped his sweaty brow.

"You can rest easy, there. I don't want too many corpses found around here or someone will get suspicious. I can come up with a pretty good alibi to tell Vivian."

A glow of relief spread over McNally's face.

"Damn, Rich, what do you think I am? I wouldn't hurt Vivian. Besides, no telling what you'd do to me if anything ever happened to her. I'll go scrounge up something to tie Lacy up with. You two have got to get out of here right away."

He was back in a minute, toting a ball of twine and a kitchen towel, which he tore into thin strips with which to bind Lacy's mouth. Then he tied her hands with the twine, showing her no mercy. With savage-like vengeance, he pulled the twine until it cut grooves into her skin. She cried out, but the sound was muffled. His knots were doubled, then doubled again. He tugged at them several times to be certain they would hold.

"Okay. That ought to do it. Get her out of here, and if she gives you any trouble after you've left the building, don't think twice about doing her in. You got a gun?"

"No."

Jim left the room, returning after a minute's absence with a large, pewter-colored revolver. "Here. Don't hesitate to use it, and don't worry about its registration. No one will be able to trace it to anyone around here."

Nodding, McNally took the gun. Then, as if on a sudden impulse, he raised the gun up over Lacy's head and with a forceful blow banged it on her crown. She slumped to the floor. Unconscious.

* * *

Lacy regained consciousness during the drive through the inky night. She was on the back floorboard of McNally's Mercedes. She tried to lift her head, but it hurt too much, so she dropped it back to its hot and bumpy resting place on the floor of the swiftly moving auto.

She must have been in a semi-conscious state throughout the ordeal of tugging her limp body out of the Capitol building because she instantly knew where she was now. She wanted to check her watch to see what time it was, to judge how much longer she would have to ride, but her hands were tied behind her.

Then it occurred to her that the longer the ride lasted the more time she would have to scheme an escape. For now, she would lie still and let McNally think she still was unconscious.

For the next twenty minutes or so, she weighed all the angles on her mental scales. Without the use of her hands, she could think of no way to escape from almost-certain death. The best plan she could come up with was to try rubbing her face on the car's carpet until the gag around her mouth slid off. Then, still pretending to be unconscious, she could wait until they were getting out of the car, then she could holler as loud as she possibly could, hoping McNally's neighbors would hear her and contact the police.

She counted while rubbing her face. By the time she got to seven hundred eighty-five, she had rubbed the torn cloth off her mouth. She kept on counting. At forty-two hundred seventy, the car turned off the main thoroughfare they had been on. Lacy judged by the bumpy ride the road they had turned on was not paved. After only a minute, McNally turned again. This time to the left. She started counting again. One, two, three, four..

By the time she got to thirty-four, the car rounded still another corner. After nosing its way perhaps ten feet, the car stopped.

Lacy shook all over. This would be her only chance, she told herself. One quick charge from the revolver could silence her permanently. She knew she had to take the risk. Once Pete got there, it would all be over.

As soon as the motor died, McNally opened the car door and sprang to his feet.

"Lacy?"

She made no reply, trying all the while to

breath in a rhythmic, even pattern which would lead him to believe she was still unconscious.

With the car door still open, he leaned into the back seat to lift up the bulk of her body. Forcing herself to go limp all over, Lacy allowed McNally to lift her off the floorboard.

As soon as her head cleared the car's doorway, she forcefully butted McNally, shoving him backward and onto the sandy ground. She screamed as loud as her voice could, and took off running.

It was then that she realized that no one could have heard her screams. No stilted houses silhouetted against the moonlit bay. McNally's bay house stood isolated on the lonely stretch of beach. She suddenly remembered Vivian McNally telling her of their wonderfully isolated bay home. Now she remembered the nearest neighbor was over a mile away. And there was no telephone.

McNally jumped to his feet and ran after her, yelling for her to stop, threatening to shoot her.

Although she was running as fast as she could, she knew she would be no match for the lithe McNally, and besides, she couldn't get enough distance between them to prevent his bullets from hitting her.

With deep reluctance, she stopped, calling out: "All right, Richard. Don't shoot."

She stood there on the wind-swept shore,

tears rolling down her cheeks. She had quit. She didn't care what happened. By now they had Mike, too. He was probably already dead. Why should she even care if she survived?

With his gun aimed at her, McNally picked his way toward her as if the ground was a sagging roof that would give way under his weight. His eyes never left Lacy.

Reaching her, he semi-circled his way to her rear, then jammed the gun into her back. "C'mon, now. Let's go up to the house. And don't try anything or I'll have to use this gun. You know, don't you, that no one could hear the shots out here. No neighbors within hearing distance."

She nodded solemnly.

They slowly walked back to the house in silence.

Set some fifty yards back from the McNally's boat dock, the house loomed up on stilts to prevent its washing away as well as to provide a better view of the Gulf.

The only access to the house was by a steep stairway which brought them to a sundeck running the length of the house. Several pair of French windows opened on to the sundeck. Those doors had to be the only entrance to the house.

When they went through the first door, Lacy glanced around and saw that the house was actually a large square, roughly divided into quarters. In one half was the living room and large kitchen, in the other a bunk room and the bath-dressing room.

He motioned for her to take a seat on a white sailcloth sofa.

"Richard, you can put the gun back in your pocket. I can't possibly get it out of your pocket, and unless I'd like to risk a twenty foot drop out of one of the windows, the only way I could get out would be through the front door. I'm not foolish enough to think I could walk right out without you shooting me."

He said nothing but put the gun into his pocket.

"Tell me, Richard. Have you ever killed anyone?"

He didn't answer for a minute. "I haven't pulled the trigger, but I have knowingly let some people who posed a threat to our organization be killed. The stupidest, most senseless murder or all was Ruth Chambers. She would have divorced him and never said a word about his corruption—she was simple minded. But he insisted on killing her. I was against that. I'd never have anyone killed unless it was a him-or-me situation, like with you. If you talk, I sit in prison for the rest of my life."

Her mind raced on. He could have shot her in the back as she ran away, but he didn't. He could have shot her as she stood on the beach, but he didn't. She realized now that he would shoot her if there was no other way to stop her, but otherwise, he would prefer to wait for Pete to arrive and take charge of the dirty job.

At least she had time on her side. How long would it take Pete to get there? They had called San Antonio at about midnight. He could have reached Austin by one. How long had it taken them to reach the bay?

"Richard?"

"Hum?"

"What time is it?"

He looked at his wristwatch. "Four in the morning. Why? You got an appointment?"

"I have a rendezvous with death." That was a corny thing to say, she thought, but she had already said it.

McNally glanced down at the floor.

"How close are you and Jim?"

"Thick as blood."

"How well do you trust him?"

"Oh, no, you don't. That won't work. Jim and I could never double cross each other. I couldn't operate without him, and he can't operate without me. I handle everything for him."

"I don't understand how you ever got mixed up in this. When you were in the Legislature you had a flawless reputation as a great legislator, and I thought you were financially independent. I know Jim got obsessed with the desire to grab for all the wealth and power he could. But you..."

"I lost everything I had on the stock market. My broker messed me up. Oh, sure, I still had some money left, but not enough to live off a legislator's seven-thousand-a-year salary. And I couldn't let Vivian readjust her standard of living.

"Actually, it all started rather modestly. I knew Jim was going places, and I made a proposition to him. I told him I'd be his chief administrative aide. He was looking for someone with legislative experience who would know all the money-men in the state. I had the right connections, and since we both needed money, we sort of made a pact to divvy up all the ill-gotten money we could make by using his office as a springboard. We started with fixing up bids and contracts. Soon, we learned that if we could delve a little in blackmailing, we could achieve much more."

She snorted. "Financially."

"Yep. We made a great deal of money off that law we passed requiring every car in the state to have that certain type of pollution-free muffler. No one ever found out that Jim and I owned controlling interest in the company which manufactured the mufflers. Reporters tried hard enough, but of course, some of our key people front for us. Then, much later than that we had to start having people killed."

He stopped again, gulping. He reminded Lacy of a drowning man, coming up for air before going down again. He had to stop for second wind before he could continue, before he could tell her that he was responsible for a person's death.

"Lacy, I had to do it. The first one was Senator Welding. We'd been blackmailing him. His was innocent enough. We knew that he had had his sister on the state payroll for handling some secretarial duties for him. It was only for a few months, but it is against state law for legislators' relatives to work for the state. He told us that as soon as he had found out, she quit. We convinced him that his constituents wouldn't believe it. Told him we might get the Travis County DA to press charges against him if he didn't play ball with us. He did. Temporarily. Then he decided to come clean. He said he had enough faith in his constituents to re-elect him after all the mess had cleared the air. He said he was going to expose us and clean up the state."

"So you had to kill him."

"We didn't have any choice." His voice almost broke."He was a really nice guy, too."

Lacy clearly remembered Senator Welding's death. It had been made to look like murder-suicide. She realized now that Welding and his wife both knew about Jim's organization. They both had to be killed. Police deduced that Welding had shot his wife, than committed suicide. Those who knew the couple were deeply shocked.

Ironically, Jim Chambers had delivered the eulogy at the double funeral.

"And what was your part in it? Was it you or Jim who gave the order?"

"Jim. But I may as well have done it. I didn't try to prevent it."

"Tell me, will you sit back and say and do nothing when Jim has Vivian killed?"

"I know what you're trying to do. It's not going to work. So kindly shut up."

He strolled across the room and turned on a CD of soft rock music.

It reminded her that only a few hours earlier she and Mike had driven along the eerie stretch of highway between San Antonio and Austin, and the music had provided the necessary catalyst to pick up her descending spirits. But nothing could do that now.

"I don't want any more talking," McNally said. Why don't you lie down there until Pete..." He trailed off. "Just stay there and shut up."

"Why don't you say it, Richard? Say *stay there until Pete, your executioner, arrives*. You can't say it, can you?"

He stood there shaking his head. "I'm sorry, Lacy. Believe me. I've always liked you, but it's the only way."

"No, Richard, I don't think it's the only way. You're an attorney. Surely you know that if you turn state's evidence you could probably get off with a very light jail term."

"There's more to it than that. What do you think it would do to Vivian if she knew what I was involved in? I'd die before I'd let her know."

"You mean to tell me she has absolutely no suspicions?"

"None whatsoever."

"Don't you think she will after tonight?"

"I can trust Jim to think of a pretty good story. When it comes to the art of chicanery, he's the greatest."

"You better just hope he comes up with something good."

"I meant it when I told you to please be quiet. I don't want to talk anymore about anything."

He walked again toward the kitchen, looking back every couple of seconds to make sure she wasn't trying to head for the French doors. He got some ice from the refrigerator and a bottle of bourbon and a hot Coke from under the kitchen sink, and he mixed two drinks.

"Here, drink this, it'll soothe your nerves," he told her as he handed a drink with a tall straw to her.

"How thoughtful of you to furnish the straw," she said sarcastically, "since you won't untie me." She sipped her drink. She really wasn't in the mood to be soothed. She wanted to think clearly, to think of a way to get out. Her only hope in getting out would be to escape from this house, but how could she do that when he had a gun? And just getting the door open would be impossible without the use of her hands.

She gave a bitter laugh to herself. *I'm going to die.*

The kitchen clock read four-thirty. Pete could be here in less than an hour if Jim had dispatched him as soon as he arrived in Austin. Of course, he could have been delayed—if he had to take care of Mike.

Mike dead. It was a paralyzing, horrifying thought. *Mike.* A modern day knight. More precious than life.

She hated Jim and McNally more than ever now for depriving her and Mike of what could have been. Facing death would have been easier had she been allowed her heaven on earth with Mike.

She pictured Mike, tall and lean, just as he had looked standing across the room from her at the Casa Rio Mexican restaurant. Her stomach gave a little jump now, just thinking of him, in the same way it had done then.

When was then? Only a day and a half ago. It seemed a century.

She sat there, sipping her drink until it was half gone. She had the illusion of being fixed in one spot as the room around her revolved. She braced herself as she sat on the sofa. She felt as if she might fall off.

Then she realized what McNally had done to her.

"Richard!" The name from her own lips sounded ridiculous. It wasn't her voice. It sounded as if she were calling through a huge tin cylinder.

"Yes, Lacy, I put something in your drink to help calm you down. I'd prefer it if you'd sleep until Pete comes—and after he gets here, too. I detest hysterical women."

Chapter 19

Lacy desperately fought the drug. After all, she told herself, she had drunk only half of the drink. Since McNally made it clear he would not tolerate a hysterical female, she had no desire to let him know she wasn't yet unconscious. She sat on the sofa in a stiff, almost lifeless position, determined all the while not to twitch a muscle.

But she could not bring herself to let the light out, so she sat there, rigid, with her expressionless eyes wide open.

To keep her mind alert, she tested herself in arithmetic. One and one are two. Two and two are four, and on until she got to the point where she couldn't go on without aid of a pencil and paper or calculator. Then, she switched to a narration of her life's memories, starting with the first. She remembered very little of her childhood. She remembered family holidays, a smattering of some of her later school teachers. Then, she remembered high school vividly, but no one incident seemed to stand out in her memory. It wasn't until she got to college that her life seemed to become a series of incidents.

Wherever her thoughts strayed, they kept coming back to Mike Talamino. She clearly recalled the circumstances surrounding their first meeting. She had met him in the law library where she was doing research for her libel course. The chivalrous young law student had come to her rescue, helping her find the right books and volunteering to help her prepare briefs. They had seen each other exclusively after that. She remembered their first kiss so vividly she could almost feel his warm lips on hers.

She remembered how he looked then and how little the years had changed him. It was while she was thinking of him that she saw his face through the window facing the sundeck not ten feet from where McNally stood.

McNally's back was to the window.

At first sight of Mike, her heart jumped.

Then when she looked back again and he wasn't there, she began to doubt her senses. Under the diffusing effects of the drug, she really could not be sure of what she saw. She could easily be hallucinating herself a savior, and since she had been thinking of Mike, there was no better candidate.

It would have been difficult for her or McNally to have heard any light noises, such as a stealthy climb of the stairs, over the music from the CD player. She wanted to believe Mike was on the sundeck waiting to save her. If he were, though, why didn't he act? She waited a few more minutes. Still nothing.

As she tried to console herself, a flurry of footsteps barged up the stairs. Footsteps of a single person—probably a woman, since they were light. Then a frantic knocking at the door followed.

"Richard, it's Vivian. Let me in."

McNally gave a quick jerk, then raced to the door. Just prior to opening the door, he tucked the gun at his waist.

When the door snapped open, a tall, huskily built man cut in between McNally and his wife, his gun drawn. "Hands up, McNally. I'm with the FBI, and you're under arrest."

At that same moment, two more armed men dashed into the room.

One of them was Mike. His eyes locked with Lacy's. "Thank God you're here. And alive."

McNally was surrounded. With tears brimming in his eyes, he lifted his arms over his head. The man accompanying Mike searched McNally and removed the gun from his midriff, while the other agent informed McNally of his rights.

There was such a whirl of activity, Lacy barely noticed Vivian standing near the doorway, weeping.

Mike came to stand in front of Lacy. "Anyone else here?"

She shook her head.

A look of deep concern crossed his face, and he immediately buried her in his embrace. "Are you okay?" he asked, his voice tender.

She nodded. "I'm okay. Really I am. It's just that Richard put something in my drink."

The two agents had not taken their eyes off McNally, nor had they quit pointing their guns at him. They apparently had no handcuffs with them.

Mike picked up his gun again and slowly stepped over to McNally. With hatred in his eyes, he thrust his gun almost within McNally's grasp as he aimed it directly at McNally's face. "What did you put in her drink?" Before giving McNally time to answer, he continued, "If this girl dies, you will too."

With his hands still overhead, McNally said, "I swear all I put in her drink was something to make her sleep for a while. Here," he started to tuck his hand into his breast when Mike shouted, "Stop it! Don't try anything."

McNally stretched his hands back toward the ceiling. "In my pocket," he motioned with his eyes toward his shirt pocket, "you'll find the powders I put in her drink. They're harmless."

Mike removed the plastic bottle from

McNally's pocket, walked to the kitchen and drew a glass of water. He approached Vivian McNally.

"What do you say, McNally," Mike said, "to letting your wife have one of harmless tablets?" He held the pill out to her.

Red eyed, she looked up at her husband questioningly. McNally's voice cracked as he spoke. "Viv, I love you so much. I never meant to hurt you." He turned from her to Mike, his voice gathering its natural strength. "If you want her to sleep, let her have it. I swear, even if my word doesn't mean much, they're harmless."

Vivian McNally drew a deep breath and moved to her husband's side. Instead of pumping her now-broken husband and chiding him for his illegal deeds, she silently stroked his back.

In all the excitement it seemed everyone, including Lacy, had forgotten her plight. Her hands still were tied behind her, and the tightly-drawn twine cut away at her raw wrists.

Mike finally took a knife from the kitchen drawer and cut her loose. When he saw her wounds, his brows drew together, and he cursed at McNally.

Although the other two men kept a close watch on McNally, they also watched Lacy and Mike. The larger of the two gave a scornful expression at Lacy's mangled wrist.

"Are you okay except for that?" Mike asked.

She nodded. "How did you get out of your car theft charges?"

"Oh, you knew about that, did you?"

"Jim found out when he called Capitol security to get you. Seems they already had you."

"Yeah. Right in the middle of my heart attack some guy says, *Ok, Buster, your gig is up. I'm placing you under arrest for the theft of Senator Marshall's car.* I nearly did have a heart attack then."

Lacy smiled.

"I didn't completely trust the Capitol guards—afraid they might be too close to Chambers—so, I thought I'd oblige and go down to the police station where I could demand to see the FBI agents. And Eddie and Jacob came down to the station and vouched for my credibility—we've worked together before. I gave them the gist of the case, and they backed me one hundred percent."

Eddie eyed Lacy, a smile on his face. "We woke up Judge Gonzales to issue a search warrant, and I think we found enough in Chambers' office to hang him. There's plenty of stuff to go through still, but our first priority was to find you."

Mike looked at Lacy and smiled. Then he put his arms around her and pulled her to his chest. "God, I'm glad you're okay."

"I'm glad *you're* okay. Jim sent a guy

named Bernie to kill you when you left the police station."

One of the agents' gaze shifted from Lacy to Mike. "Sounds like still another charge against Chambers."

Mike nodded. "And I guess you two scared old Bernie off."

"How'd you find me here?" Lacy asked.

"Blind luck, I guess." Mike smiled and seized her hand.

"Jim wouldn't tell, huh?"

Mike shrugged. "We haven't talked to him yet. Not able to find him. He wasn't in his apartment. We got Mrs. McNally when she tried the knob to Chambers' apartment. She told us about the phone call. She said she had been concerned over her husband and had tried to call Chambers' number but kept getting a busy signal."

Vivian addressed her husband. "What happened to your cell?"

"Jim made me turn it off."

"I was worried to death about you," she said, hitching a sob. "With good reason, apparently."

"By that time we had men all over town, and none of them could turn up any helpful information on Chambers' whereabouts," Eddie said. "The highway patrol, though, saw a car meeting the description of McNally's Mercedes heading out of town on Highway 290. We asked Mrs. McNally if she knew of any place in the direction of 290 her husband might be. She suggested this place and came along to show us the way."

Terror struck Lacy as swiftly as a sudden kick. "You mean to tell me that Jim hasn't been apprehended yet?"

"There's an all-points bulletin out for him right now, but as of yet, he hasn't been located."

Her face lost its color, her lashes lowered, then she snapped back, her voice more strident. "My God, they know we're here. Jim was to send the redhead here to kill me. He may be close."

The taller of the two agents took a short step toward Lacy. "Don't worry. We'll protect you."

"By the way, Lace, this is my friend Eddie," Mike said, nodding at the taller agent. Then his glance skipped to the other agent. "And this is Special Agent Jacob Miller."

She thanked them.

Mike turned his attention to McNally. "You know, McNally, your wife was a tremendous help to us. Of course, she had no idea you could possibly be mixed up in this sordid mess. She was convinced you were the innocent bystander. It's to your credit that she aided the FBI. It will also be to your credit if you cooperate with us. If you can help us get a conviction against Chambers, we may be able to get you off with a very light sentence."

McNally nodded.

"It's also to your credit that Lacy wasn't killed." Mike turned to Jacob. "I'd feel better if you stand out on the deck—in case the hit man shows up."

The door burst open. "Too late." The voice was Jim's. Everyone turned as he and Pete stormed into the room. Pete dove at Mike and brought him down.

Jim grabbed Lacy and jammed his gun to her temple. A third man came through the doorway and aimed his gun on the agents who had been guarding McNally.

Jim butted the gun into Lacy's skull. "Throw your guns over here, or she gets it."

They obliged, tossing the guns toward the man Lacy presumed was Bernie. Pete and Mike had been struggling until Mike realized Lacy's peril.

Jim looked down at him. "Get up, Talamino, and put your hands over your head, or I'll kill Lacy."

Mike rose immediately. Pete took his gun but still frisked him until he was certain Mike was disarmed, then told him to stand by the other captives.

For the second time in one night, Lacy faced death. This time she was somewhat more composed. "Jim, you must have heard Mike just before you came in when he said police all over the state are looking for you. It would be to your advantage to come clean, to cooperate with the FBI."

"Wrong, Baby. We're going to take Richard's boat to Mexico. It will be much better if we don't leave pointing fingers like the lot of you behind." He looked at McNally. "I've taken all our ready cash from your office safe and made a few phone calls to raise some more. How much fuel do you have for the boat?"

"Since this place is so isolated, I always keep a surplus of gas. We've got enough to get down into Mexico."

Jim nodded, then called McNally over. McNally stopped to retrieve his gun, then the two men spoke in muffled tones. After a brief conversation, McNally walked toward the door.

"I better go check on the boat," McNally said as he walked outside.

"May I sit now?" Lacy asked Jim.

He nodded.

She sat on the couch. Opposite her, Mike and the others remained standing, while Pete and the other man aimed guns at the three men. Vivian had taken a seat at the glass-topped dining table.

Jim backed up to where he could see Lacy and the others in the same glance. "Pete?" he called.

"Huh?"

"What do you think is the best way to get

rid of them?"

"At sea."

Jim nodded. "Bernie, maybe you'd better go check Richard."

"Whatever you say, Gov." He kept his gun out as he left the house.

As soon as he stepped from the house, several shots were fired. It sounded as if they came from the sundeck.

At the instant Jim's gaze flicked toward the door, Mike dove at him. Jim's gun went off, grazing Mike's forearm.

Screams ripped from Lacy and Vivian.

Despite that Mike's blood was spewing, he grabbed Jim and knocked the gun from his hand. But Jim was much bigger. Much stronger. He locked his arms around Mike, shoving him into the tile floor and bashing Mike's head repeatedly into the floor.

The door snapped open. McNally burst into the room and blasted Pete with gunfire.

Jim let go of Mike and went for his gun.

McNally turned his gun on Jim, but he wasn't quick enough. Jim had already pulled the trigger.

They shot each other simultaneously.

Although he'd lost a good bit of blood, Mike managed to get Jim's gun as the latter fell to the ground, his bloody hands splaying over the wound to his chest.

Jim lost consciousness.

Lacy's gaze shifted to Pete. A bullet had

pierced his forehead. She quickly looked away.

Mike dropped to one knee and felt for Jim's pulse, fingering it for a few minutes. Then he looked up at Lacy. "He's gone."

The whole bloody scene had put her almost in a daze. Her glance fanned from Mike and Jim to the McNallys.

Vivian had rushed to her husband's side, but he was unable to talk. He lay in a pool of his own blood. Seizing her hand, he tried to speak. Vivian gripped his hand firmly and sobbed. Soon, his hand went limp.

Vivian screamed a horrible wail as if the life had been pulled from her own body.

The two agents helped her to the sofa where they wrapped a blanket around her. "She's in shock," Jacob said, his voice low and reverent.

Lacy had sprung to her feet to help Mike. "Could you guys get something to help stop Mike's bleeding?" She squatted beside him and lifted his wounded arm.

Eddie came and examined Mike's arm. "Can you get me a couple of towels?" he asked Lacy.

Seconds later she was presenting him with two. He used the first to wipe away the blood while telling her to tear the second into strips.

"Here, I'll help," Jacob said, removing a Swiss Army knife from his pocket.

After Eddie cleaned the wound, he used the

strips Jacob had cut to bind the arm. "I hope this will stem the flow of blood." He stood and looked at Mike. "Well, Talamino, you won't be pitching in any softball games for a while." His glance darted to Lacy. "You better get him to a hospital." He tossed her a set of keys. "Take my car. It's the gray one."

Then he addressed Jacob. "Call Austin and have them send us help."

Eddie helped Mike to his feet. "You're going to be OK."

Before Lacy and Mike left, Lacy silently embraced Vivian. What words could she possibly utter?

Lacy and Mike walked out into the dawn arm in arm.

"I'm driving," Lacy announced. "For once, I'm going to take care of you."

"Maybe this once, but from now on, I'm planning to take care of you."

Her heartbeat stampeded. "Like a policeman or--" She faltered and gazed at his moonlit face, the face of the man she loved. "Or a husband?"

"I thought—I hoped—as your husband."

Tears stung her eyes as she nodded. "For the record, I love you. I never stopped loving you. And I'll never let you get away from me again, Michael Talamino. My hero."

The End

Texas Heroines in Peril

If you enjoyed reading *Capitol Offense,* you may also enjoy the other three installments of *Texas Heroines in Peril:*

Protecting Britannia
(Texas Heroines in Peril Series)

"Drawing on her real-life expertise as a dealer in British antiques, Cheryl Bolen pens a fast-paced, fascinating tale of modern-day romantic suspense." – *Colleen Thompson, Rita finalist romantic suspense*

"It's fun to watch the case unfold in this nonstop action adventure. 4 Stars" – *Romantic Times magazine*

* * *

Antiques dealer Britannia Hensley's first day back in London after a seven-year absence seems like an audition for a Survivor in the City episode. Her plane arrives two hours late; she sloshes through blinding rain without an umbrella; her purse is snatched; her hotel room ransacked; some slimeball jabs a gun into her back and tries to abduct her; and every bobby in London's after her for a murder she didn't commit. What's a girl to do when she has no passport, no money, no means of getting any money, and no one she can call? Well, actually there is someone . . . but surely after all these years a handsome guy like Graham's been snatched up by some lucky girl.

Murder at Veranda House
(Texas Heroines in Peril Series)

Lovely young widow Annette Holcombe is forced to turn her Veranda House on Galveston Island into a B & B after the recent death of her husband, a man she'd known only a short time. Upon his untimely death, she learns that the only thing she really knew about him was that everything she knew about him was a lie!

And if being penniless wasn't bad enough, now Annette's got to contend with threatening letters, suspicious guests, fears for her daughter's safety, an impending hurricane—and murder! If only there was someone to trust. Someone like Dr. Grant Garrison, a personable, good-looking guest who's teaching at the island's medical school.

But Grant, too, isn't what he seems.

A Cry in the Night
(Texas Heroines in Peril Series)

The child she gave up for adoption eight years ago is missing, and Ava Simpson is convinced his life is in danger. Only one person can help her find the boy: Blake Tranowski, the birth father of the child. If only she can forge the courage to tell him of the existence of their son. . .

The anger Blake felt toward Ava when she dumped him nine years ago can't touch the fury he experiences when she makes her shattering revelation. Even more shattering is Blake's discovery that the boy really has gone missing. Why hasn't the adoptive father contacted the police? How is the man involved with a Mexican drug cartel? Is their son even alive? As Blake and Ava race against the clock to find their son, others are intent on stopping them. Even if it means killing them.

Author's Biography

A former journalist who, in her own words, has "a fascination with dead Englishwomen," Cheryl Bolen is the award-winning author of more than a dozen historical romance novels set in Regency England, including *Marriage of Inconvenience*, *My Lord Wicked*, and *A Duke Deceived*. Her books have received numerous awards, such as the 2011 International Digital Award for Best Historical Novel and the 2006 Holt Medallion for Best Historical. She was also a 2006 finalist in the Daphne du Maurier for Best Historical Mystery. Her works have been translated into eleven languages and have been Amazon.com bestsellers. Bolen has contributed to *Writers Digest* and *Romance Writers Report* as well as to the Regency era–themed newsletters *The Regency Plume, The Regency Reader*, and *The Quizzing Glass*. The mother of two grown sons, she lives with her professor husband in Texas.